The
END OF
SUMMER

The
END OF
SUMMER

ROSAMUNDE
PILCHER

St. Martin's Press

Printed in the United States of America

ISBN   0-440-20255-8

The
END OF
SUMMER

Chapter 1

ALL SUMMER LONG the weather had been heavy and clouded, the warmth of the sun blanketed by sea fogs which had continually rolled in from the Pacific. But by September, as so often happens in California, the fogs retreated, far out into the ocean, where they lay along the edge of the horizon, sullen as a long bruise.

Inland, beyond the coastal range, farmlands, heavy with crops, with bursting fruit, and corn and artichokes, and orange pumpkins, simmered in the sunshine. Small wooden townships dozed, skewered by the heat, grey and dusty as specimen moths. The plains, rich and fertile, stretched east to the foothills of the Sierra Nevada, and through it all arrowed the great freeway of the Camino Real, north to San Francisco, and south to Los Angeles, crammed and glittering with the hot steel of a million cars.

Through the summer months, the beach had been deserted, for Reef Point was the end of the line and seldom patronized by the casual day tripper. For one thing, the road was unsurfaced, unsafe, and uninviting. For another, the little resort of La Carmella, with its charming tree-shaded streets, exclusive country club and spotless motels, lay just over the point, and anyone with sense and a few dollars to spare, stayed put right there. Only if you were adventurous, or broke, or surfing mad, did you risk the last mile and come slipping and scrambling over the dirt track that led down to this great, empty, storm-washed bay.

But now, with the fine hot weather and the clean rolling breakers pouring up on to the beach, the place flowered with people. Cars of all sorts came tumbling down the hill, to park in the shade beneath the cedars, and disgorge picnickers, campers, surfers and whole families of hippies, newly wearied of San Francisco, and heading south for New Mexico and the sun, like so many migrating birds. And the weekends brought the University students up from Santa Barbara in their old convertibles and their flower-stickered Volkswagens, all packed with girls and crates of canned beer, and hung about with the big brightly-coloured Malibu surf boards. They set up little camps all over the beach and the air was full of their voices and laughter, and the smell of sun oil.

And so, after weeks and months of being virtually on our own, we were surrounded by people and every sort of activity. My father was hard at work, trying to write a script to a deadline, and in an impossible frame of mind. Unnoticed by him, I moved out on to the beach, taking sustenance with me (hamburgers and Coca-Cola), a book to read, a large bath-towel for comfort and Rusty for company.

Rusty was a dog. My dog. A brown woolly thing of indeterminate breed, but great intelligence. When we first moved to the cabin, back in the spring, we hadn't got a dog, and Rusty, spying us, had decided to remedy this. Accordingly he hung around. I chased him off, shooed him away, Father threw old boots at him, still he returned, un-repentant and bearing no malice at all, to sit a yard or two from the back porch, smiling and thumping away with his tail. One hot morn-ing, taking pity on him, I gave him a bowl of cool water to drink. He lapped it clean, then sat down and smiled and started thumping again. The next day, I gave him an old ham bone, which he took politely, removed, buried, and was back again in five minutes. Smiling. Thump, thump, went the tail.

My father came out of the house and threw a boot at him, but without much enthusiasm. It was simply a half-hearted show of force. Rusty knew this and moved in a little nearer.

I said to my father, "Who do you suppose he belongs to?"

"God knows."

"He seems to think he belongs to us."

"You're wrong," said my father. "He thinks we belong to him."

"He's not fierce or anything and he doesn't smell."

He looked up from the magazine he was trying to read. "Are you trying to say you want to keep the bloody thing?"

"It's just that I don't see . . . I don't see how we're going to get rid of him."

"Short of shooting him."

"Oh, don't."

"He'll have fleas. Bring fleas into the house."

"I'll buy him a flea collar." Father watched me over his spectacles. I could see he was beginning to laugh. I said, "Please. Why not? He'll be company for me while you're away."

Father said, "All right," so I put on some shoes, then and there, and whistled up the dog, and walked over the hill into La Carmella where there is a very fancy vet's, and there I waited in a little room filled with pampered poodles and Siamese cats, and their various owners, and at last I was let in, and the vet looked at Rusty and pronounced him fit, and gave him an injection, and told me where I could buy a flea collar. So I paid the vet and went out and bought the flea collar, and we walked home again. We came into the house, and Father was still reading his magazine, and the dog came politely in, and after standing around a little, waiting to be asked to sit down, he sat, on the old rug in front of the empty fireplace.

My father said, "What's his name?" and I said, "Rusty," because I'd once had a dog-nightdress-case called Rusty and it was the first name that came into my head.

There was no question of his fitting into the family, because it seemed that he had always belonged. Wherever I went, Rusty came too. He loved the beach, and was forever digging up splendid treasures and bringing them home for us to admire. Old bits of flotsam, plastic detergent bottles, long dangling strips of seaweed. And sometimes things that he had obviously not dug up. A new sneaker, a bright bathtowel, and once a punctured beach-ball, which my father had to replace once I had run its small and weeping owner to earth. He liked to swim too, and always insisted on accompanying me, although I could swim much faster and farther than he could, and he was always tagging behind. You'd have thought he'd have got discouraged, but he never did.

We had been swimming that day, a Sunday. Father, the deadline met, had driven down to Los Angeles to deliver the script in person, and Rusty and I had kept each other company, in and out of the sea all afternoon, gathering shells, playing with an old stick of driftwood. But now it was getting cooler and I had put some clothes on again, and we sat, side by side, the setting sun gold and blinding in our eyes, watching the surfers.

They had been at it all day, but it seemed that they would never tire. Kneeling on their boards, they paddled out to sea, through the breakers to the smooth green water beyond. There they waited, patient, perched on the skyline like so many cormorants, waiting for the swell to gather, to form and finally break. They chose a wave, stood as the water curved up and crested and showed white at its edge, and as it curled over and thundered in, so the surfers came too, riding across the wave, a poem of balance, arrogant with the confidence of youth; riding the wave until it swept up on to the sand, and then stepping casually off, and gathering up the board, and back into the sea again, for the surfer's creed is that there is always a bigger and a better comber, just around the corner, and now the sun was setting and it would soon be dark, and there was not a moment to be lost.

One boy in particular had caught my eye. He was blond, crew cut, very brown, his skinny knee-length shorts the same bright blue as his surf board. He was a wonderful surfer, with a style and a dash that made all the others look clumsy amateurs. But now, as I watched, he seemed to decide to call it a day, for he rode in on a final wave, beached himself neatly, stepped off the board, and with a final long look at the rose-washed evening sea, turned and picked up the surf board and began to walk in up the sand.

I looked away. He came close beside me, and then went on a few yards to where a pile of neatly folded clothes had been waiting. He dropped the surf board and picked up a faded college sweat shirt from the top of the pile. I glanced his way again, and as his face came out of the opening at the top of the sweat shirt, he looked straight at me. Firmly, I met his eye.

He seemed amused. He said, "Hi."

"Hello."

He settled the sweat shirt down over his hips. He said, "Want a cigarette?"

"All right."

He stooped and took a packet of Luckys and a lighter out of a pocket and came over the sand to where I was sitting, and he flipped a cigarette up for me and took one himself and lit them both, and then let himself down beside me, stretching full length and leaning back on his elbows. His legs and his neck and his hair were all lightly dusted with sand, and he had blue eyes and that clean, well-scrubbed look still to be seen on the campuses of American Universities.

He said, "You've been sitting there all afternoon. When you weren't swimming."

"I know."

"Why didn't you join us?"

"I haven't got a surf board."

"You could get one."

"No money."

"Then borrow one."

"There's no one I know to borrow one from."

The young man frowned. "You're British, aren't you?"

"Yes."

"You visiting?"

"No, I live here."

"In Reef Point?"

"Yes." I jerked my head, indicating the line of faded clapboard cabins visible just over the curve of the sand dunes.

"How'd you come to live here?"

"We rented the cabin."

"Who's we?"

"My father and I."

"How long have you been here?"

"Since spring."

"But you're not staying over the winter."

It was a statement of fact more than a question. Nobody stayed in Reef Point over the winter. The houses weren't built to withstand the storms, the access road became impassable, the telephone lines blew down, the electricity failed.

"I think so. Unless we decide to move on."

He frowned. "Are you hippies, or something?"

Knowing how I looked at the time, I kindly did not blame him for asking this question.

"No. But my father writes film scripts and stuff for TV. But he hates Los Angeles so much he refuses to live there, so . . . we rented this cabin."

He seemed intrigued. "And what do you do?"

I took up a handful of sand, let it run away, coarse and grey through my fingers.

"Nothing much. Buy food and empty the garbage can and try to keep the sand swept out of the house."

"Is that your dog?"

"Yes."

"What's his name?"

"Rusty."

"Rusty. Hey, Rusty, fella!" Rusty acknowledged his advances with a nod that would have done credit to Royalty and then continued to gaze out to sea. To make up for his lack of manners I said, "Are you from Santa Barbara?"

"Uh-huh." But the young man did not want to talk about himself. "How long have you lived in the States? You still have a terribly terribly British accent."

I smiled politely at a joke heard many times before. "Since I was fourteen. Seven years."

"In California?"

"All over. New York. Chicago. San Francisco."

"Is your father American?"

"No. He just likes it here. He came in the first place because he wrote a novel, and it was bought by a film company and he came to Hollywood to write the script."

"No kidding? Have I heard of him? What's his name?"

"Rufus Marsh."

"You mean, *Tall as the Morning?*" I nodded. "Boy, I read that cover to cover, when I was still in high school. I got all my sex education out of that book." He looked at me with new interest, and I thought that this was how it always was. They were friendly and quite kind, but never interested until I mentioned *Tall as the Morning.* I suppose it had something to do with the way I look, because my eyes are pale as sixpences, and my lashes are quite colourless, and my face doesn't go brown but gets splashed and splattered with hundreds of enormous freckles. Besides that, I am too tall for a girl, and the bones in my face all show. "He must be quite a guy."

A new expression had come into his face, puzzled, and crossed with questions that he was obviously going to be too polite to ask.

If you are Rufus Marsh's daughter, how come you're sitting on this god-forsaken beach in the back woods of California wearing patched jeans and a man's shirt that should have been relegated to the rag bag decades ago, and you haven't even got enough dollars raked together to buy yourself a surf board?

He said, following with laughable predictability the line of my own reflections, "What kind of a man is he, anyway? I mean, apart from being a father."

"I don't know." I could never describe him, even to myself. I took another handful of sand, trickled it into a miniature mountain, stubbed my cigarette out on its apex, forming a little crater, a tiny volcano, with a cigarette stub as its smoking core. A man who must always be on the move. A man who makes friends easily and loses them the next day. A quarrelsome, argumentative man, talented to the point of genius, but utterly baffled by the small problems of day-to-day living. A man who can charm and infuriate. A paradox of a man.

I said again, "I don't know," and turned to look at the boy beside me. He was nice. "I'd ask you home for a beer, and then you could meet him and see for yourself. But he's in Los Angeles just now, won't be home until tomorrow morning."

He considered this, scratching thoughtfully at the back of his head and dislodging a small storm of sand.

"Tell you what," he said, "I'm coming back next weekend if the weather holds."

I smiled. "Are you?"

"I'll look out for you."

"All right."

"I'll bring a spare board. You can surf."

I said, "You don't need to bribe me."

He pretended to be offended. "Whaddya mean, bribe?"

"I'll take you up to meet him next weekend. He likes new faces around the place."

"I wasn't bribing. Honest."

I relented. Besides, I wanted to surf. I said, "I know."

He grinned and stubbed out the cigarette. The sun, sinking towards the edge of the sea, was taking shape and colour—an orange pumpkin of a sun. He sat up, screwing his eyes against its glare, yawned slightly and stretched. He said, "I must go," and stood up and then hesitated for a moment, standing over me. His shadow seemed to stretch forever. "Goodbye then."

" 'Bye."

"Next Sunday."

"O.K."

"That's a date. Don't forget."

"I won't."

He turned and moved off, stopping to collect the rest of his gear, and turning to sketch a final salute before walking away, the length of the beach, to where the old sand-buried cedars marked the track that led up to the road.

I watched him go, and realized that I didn't even know his name.

7

And, worse, he hadn't bothered to ask mine. I was simply Rufus Marsh's daughter. But still, next Sunday, if the weather held, he would maybe be back. If the weather held. That was always something to look forward to.

Chapter 2

IT WAS BECAUSE of Sam Carter that we were living at Reef Point. Sam was my father's agent in Los Angeles, and it was in sheer desperation that he eventually offered to find somewhere cheap for us to live, because Los Angeles and my father were so acutely antipathetic that not one sellable word was he able to write while we lived there, and Sam was in danger of losing both valuable clients and money.

"There's this place at Reef Point," Sam had said. "It's a one-horse set-up, but real peaceful . . . end of the world type peace," he added, conjuring up visions of a sort of Gauguin paradise.

And so we had taken a lease on the cabin, and packed all our worldly possessions, which were sadly small, into Father's old beat-up Dodge, and driven here, leaving the smog and rat-race of Los Angeles behind us, and excited as children by the first smell of the sea.

And at first, it had been exciting. After the city it was magic to wake to nothing but the sound of sea birds and the endless thunder of the surf. It was good, in the early mornings, to walk out on to sand, to watch the sun rise over the hills, to hang out a line of washing, and watch it billow and fill with the sea wind, white as new sails.

Our housekeeping was necessarily simple—I have never been much of a housekeeper anyway, and at Reef Point there was only one small shop—a drug store, but back in Scotland my grandmother would have called it a Jenny a' Thing, for it sold everything from gun licences to house frocks, from frozen foods to packets of Kleenex. It was run by Bill and Myrtle, in a half-hearted, time-consuming sort of way, for they always seemed to be clean out of fresh vegetables, fruit, chickens and eggs, which were the sort of things I wanted to buy. However, over the summer we became quite fond of tinned chile con carne and frozen pizza pie, and all the various species of ice-cream that Myrtle obviously adored, for she was enormously fat, her great hips and thighs bulging in blue jeans, and her ham-like arms fully exposed by the girlish sleeveless blouses she chose to wear with them.

But now, after six months of Reef Point, I was getting restless. This fine Indian Summer weather would last—how long? Another month, perhaps. And then the storms would start in earnest, the darkness fall earlier, the rains would come and the mud and the wind. The cabin had no sort of central heating, only the enormous fireplace in the draughty living-room, which burned driftwood at a terrifying pace. I thought of homely buckets of coal with longing, but there was no coal. Every time I came up off the beach, I lugged a spar or branch of driftwood with me, like some pioneer woman, and added it to the pile by the back porch. It was assuming vast dimensions, but I knew that once we started needing fires, it would take no time to get through the lot.

The cabin lay just back off the beach, a small rise of sand dune its only shelter from the sea winds. It was built of wood, faded to a silvery grey, and stood up on piers, so that a couple of steps led up to the front and back porches. Inside, there was a big living-room, with picture windows facing over the ocean; a tiny, narrow kitchen; a bathroom— with no bath, but a shower—and two bedrooms, one large "master" bedroom where my father slept, and a smaller one, with a bunk, perhaps intended for a small child or an unimportant elderly relative, which was mine. It was furnished in the faintly depressing manner of summer cabins, in that all the furniture had obviously been thrown out of other, and larger, houses. Father's bed was a vast brass monstrosity, missing knobs, and with a set of springs that squeaked every time he turned over. And in my room hung an ornate gilt mirror which looked as though it had started life in a Victorian bordello, and gave me back a reflection of a drowned woman covered with black spots.

The sitting-room was not much better—the old armchairs sagged, their worn patches disguised with crocheted Afghans, the hearth-rug had a hole in it, and the other chairs were stuffed horsehair with the horsehair fighting a winning battle to get out. There was only one table, and Father had taken over one end of this as a desk, so that we were forced to take our meals, cramped and with elbows jammed in, at the other end. The best thing in the house was the window seat, which took up the whole width of the room, was padded with foam and warm

rugs and cushions, and as inviting as an old nursery sofa, if you wanted
to curl up and read, or watch the sunset, or simply think.

But it was a lonely place. At night the wind nudged and whined
through the gaps around the window, and the rooms were filled with
strange rustlings and creakings, for all the world like a ship at sea.
When my father was there, none of this mattered, but when I was left
alone, my imagination, inspired by the tales of everyday violence,
culled from the columns of the local newspapers, really got to work.
The cabin itself was a fragile thing, none of the locks on the doors or
windows would have deterred a determined intruder, and now, with
the summer over, and the occupants of the other cabins packed up and
returned to their various homes, it was completely isolated. Even Myrtle and Bill were a good quarter of a mile away, and the telephone was
a party line, and not always very efficient. One way and another, the
possibilities didn't bear thinking about.

I never spoke to my father about these fears—he had, after all, a
job of work to do, and he was essentially a perceptive man, and I am
sure knew that I was capable of working myself up into a state of jitters,
and this was one of the reasons that he let me keep Rusty.

That evening, after the day on the crowded beach, the cheerful
sunshine, and my encounter with the young student from Santa Barbara, the cabin seemed doubly deserted.

The sun had slid down over the edge of the sea, an evening breeze
was stirring, and soon it would be dark, so, for company, I lit a fire,
recklessly piling on the driftwood; and, for comfort, took a hot shower,
washed my hair, and then, wrapped in a towel, went into my room for
a pair of clean jeans and an old white sweater which had belonged to
my father until I mistakenly shrank it.

Underneath the bordello mirror was a varnished chest of drawers
which had to do duty as a dressing-table. On it, for lack of anywhere
else, I had put my photographs. There were a lot of them and they
took up a lot of space, and most of the time I didn't even look at them
very much, but this evening was different, and as I combed the snarls
out of my long wet hair I studied them, one by one, as though they
belonged to a person I scarcely knew, were of places that I had never
seen.

There was my mother, a formal portrait, framed in silver. Mother
with her shoulders bare and diamonds in her ears, and her hair newly
done by Elizabeth Arden. I loved the picture, but it was not as I remembered her. This was better, an enlarged snapshot on a picnic,

wearing her tartan skirt, and sitting waist deep in heather, and laughing as though something ridiculous were about to happen. And then there was the collection—more of a montage—with which I had filled both sides of a big leather folding frame. Elvie—the old white house, set against a fold of larch and pine, the hill rising behind it, the glimmer of the loch at the end of the lawn, the jetty, and the baulky old dinghy we had used when we fished for trout. And my grandmother, at the open french windows, the inevitable pair of secateurs ready in her hand. And a coloured postcard of Elvie Loch that I had bought in the Thrumbo post office. And another picnic, with my parents together, our old car in the background, and a fat liver-and-white spaniel sitting at my mother's feet.

And there were the photographs of my cousin Sinclair. Dozens of them. Sinclair with his first trout, Sinclair dressed in his kilt, headed for some outing or other. Sinclair in a white shirt, captain of his prep school cricket team. Sinclair skiing; at the wheel of his car; wearing a paper top hat at some New Year's Eve party and looking a little drunk. (In this photograph he had his arm around a pretty, dark girl, but I had arranged the pictures so that she didn't show.)

Sinclair was the child of my mother's brother, Aylwyn. Aylwyn had married—far too young, everybody said—a girl called Silvia. The family disapproval of his choice unhappily proved well-founded, for, as soon as she had borne her young husband a baby son, she upped and left the pair of them, and went off to live with a man who sold real estate in the Balearic Islands. After the initial shock had worn off, everybody agreed that it was the best thing that could have happened, specially for Sinclair, who was handed over to his grandmother, and brought up at Elvie under the happiest of circumstances. He had always seemed, to me, to have the best of everything.

His father, my Uncle Aylwyn, I had no recollection of at all. When I was very small, he had gone to Canada, presumably returning every now and then to visit his mother and his child, but never at Elvie when we were there. My only concern with him was the possibility of his sending me a Red Indian head dress. Over the years, I must have made the suggestion a hundred times, but nothing ever came of it.

And so Sinclair was, virtually, my grandmother's child. And I could not remember a time when I hadn't been more or less in love with him. Six years older than I, he had been the mentor of my childhood, enormously wise and endlessly brave. He had taught me to tie a hook on a line, to swing upside-down on his trapeze, to bowl a cricket ball. Together we had swum and sledged, lit illegal bonfires, built a tree house, and played pirates in the leaky old boat.

When I first came to America, I wrote to him regularly, but eventually became discouraged by his lack of response. Soon our correspondence dwindled to Christmas cards, or a scribbled note on a birthday, and it was from my grandmother that I got news of him, and from her too that I had received the photograph of the New Year Party.

After my mother died, as if Sinclair on her hands was not enough, she had offered to give me a home as well.

"Rufus, why not leave the child with me?" This was just after the funeral, back at Elvie, with grief put away and the future to be discussed in her usual practical fashion. I was not meant to be listening, but I was there, on the stairs, and their voices came clearly from beyond the closed library door.

"Because one child on your hands is more than sufficient."

"But I would love to have Jane . . . and she would be company for me as well."

"Isn't that a little selfish?"

"I don't think so."

"But, Rufus, it is her life you should think about now, her future . . ."

My father said a single very rude word. I was horrified, not at the word, but because he had said it to her. I wondered if he was a little drunk. . . .

Ignoring this, in her usual ladylike fashion, my grandmother went on, but her voice was buttoned down, the way it always got when she began to be angry.

"You've just told me that you're going to America to write the film script of your book. You can't drag a fourteen-year-old all the way to Hollywood."

"Why not?"

"What about her schooling?"

"There are schools in America."

"It would be so easy for me to have her here. Just until you've settled, found yourself a place to live."

My father pushed back his chair with a scrape. I heard his feet, pacing the floor.

"And then," he said, "I send for her and you put her on the next plane?"

"Of course."

"It won't work, you know."

"Why shouldn't it work?"

"Because if I leave Jane here with you for any length of time, Elvie would become her home and she'd never want to leave it again. You know she'd rather be at Elvie than anywhere else in the world."

"Then for her sake . . ."

"For her sake, I'm taking her with me."

There was a long silence. Then my grandmother spoke again. "That isn't the only reason is it, Rufus?"

He hesitated, as though he wished not to offend her. "No," he said at last.

"With all considerations, I still think you're making a mistake."

"If I am, it's my own. Just as she's my own child and I'm holding on to her."

I had heard enough. I sprang up and ran helter-skelter up the dark staircase. In my room, face down across my bed, I burst into miserable tears, because I was leaving Elvie, because I would never see Sinclair again, and because the two people I loved most in all the world had been fighting over me.

I wrote, of course, and my grandmother replied, and Elvie with all its sounds and smells was contained in her letters. And then, after a year or two had passed, "Why don't you come back to Scotland?" she wrote. "Just for a little holiday, a month or so. We all miss you dreadfully and there is such a lot for you to see. I made a new rose border in the walled garden, and Sinclair will be up for August . . . he has a little flat in Earls Court, and gave me lunch last time I was up in town. If there is any difficulty about the fare you know you only have to say, and I shall get Mr Bembridge at the travel agent's to send you your return ticket. Talk it over with your father."

The thought of Elvie, in August, with Sinclair, was almost irresistible, but I could not talk it over with my father, because I had overheard that angry discussion in the library and I did not think that he would let me go.

Besides, it seemed that there was never the time nor the opportunity to make the journey home. It was as though we had become nomads—we arrived in a place, we settled, and then it was time to go somewhere else. Sometimes we were rich, more often broke. My father, without my mother's restraining hand, spent money like water. We lived in Hollywood mansions, in motels, in Fifth Avenue apartments, in crummy lodging houses. As the years went by, it seemed as if we had spent our whole lives travelling America, and that we should never settle down anywhere again, and the memory of Elvie faded and became unreal, as though the waters of Elvie Loch had risen and engulfed the whole place, and I had to remind myself forcibly that it was still there, peopled by living beings who were part of me, and whom I loved, and not drowned and lost forever, blurred and dimly seen through the deep waters of some terrible natural disaster.

At my ankles, Rusty whined. Startled, I looked down and for a moment, so far away had I been, I couldn't think who he was or what he was doing. And then, like a home-movie that has stuck in the middle, there was a click in the machinery, and everyday life moved on again, and I realized that my hair was nearly dry, that Rusty was hungry and wanted his dinner, and what was more, so did I. So I laid down my comb, and pushed Elvie out of my mind, and went to throw more wood on the fire, and then inspect the icebox for something that we could eat.

It was nearly nine o'clock when I heard the car come down the hill, over the track that led from La Carmella. I heard it because it came, as all cars necessarily do, in bottom gear, and because I was alone, and all my perceptions were subconsciously sharpened to catch the smallest unfamiliar sound.

I was reading a book, and in the act of turning over a page, but I froze still and pricked my ears. Rusty sensed this, and sat up immediately, very quiet, as though he did not wish to disturb anything. Together, we listened. A log slid down in the fire, the surf distantly boomed. The car came on down the hill.

I thought . . . *Myrtle and Bill. They've been to a movie, in La Carmella.* But the car didn't stop at the drug store. It came on, still grinding along in low gear, passed the cedars where the picnickers parked their cars, on along the lonely road that could lead only to me.

My father? But he wasn't due back until tomorrow night. The young man I had met today, returning for a glass of beer? A vagrant? An escaped convict? A sex maniac . . . ?

I sprang up, dropping my book on the hearth-rug, and fled to check the snibs on the doors. They were both locked. But the cabin had no curtains, anyone could look in and see me, and I wouldn't be able to see them. In a frenzy of fear, I dashed to turn off all the lights, but the fire still burned bright, and filled the living-room with flickering light . . . it played up the walls and over the furniture, giving the old chairs a brooding, pouncing look.

The approaching headlights probed the darkness outside. Now, I could see the car coming, gently, bumping over the dried ruts of the road. It passed the last empty cabin next to ours, and coasted gently to a halt right alongside our back porch. And it wasn't my father.

I whispered Rusty to my side, for the comfort of holding his flea collar and feeling the warmth of his furry brown coat. Growls and mutters went on in the back of his throat but he didn't bark. Together we heard the engine of the car being killed, then the door opened and slammed shut. Silence for a moment. Then steps came softly over the sandy ground that lay between the back porch and the road, and the next instant there was a knocking at the door.

I let out a sort of gasp and it was too much for Rusty who tore from my grip and ran, barking his head off, to get at whatever waited outside.

"Rusty!" I went after him, but he went on and on barking. "Rusty, don't do it . . . Rusty!"

I caught him by the flea collar and dragged him back from the door, but he went on barking, and it occurred to me that he sounded so large and so fierce that this was possibly the best thing that could have happened.

I pulled myself together, gave him a shake which finally silenced him, and then straightened up. My shadow, thrown by the firelight, danced against the locked door.

I swallowed, took a deep breath and said in a voice as firm and clear as I could make it:

"Who is it?"

A man spoke. "I'm sorry to disturb you, but I'm looking for Mr Marsh's house."

A friend of Father's? Or just a trick to get in? I hesitated.

He spoke again.

"Is this where Rufus Marsh lives?"

"Yes, it is."

"Is he at home?"

Another trick?

"Why?" I said.

"Well, I was told I might find him here." I was still trying to decide what to do when he added, in quite a different voice, "Is that Jane?"

There is nothing more disarming than having a stranger know your name. Besides, there was something about his voice . . . even blurred as it was through the tightly closed door . . . something . . .

I said, "Yes."

"Is your father there?"

"No, he's in Los Angeles. Who are you?"

"Well, my name's David Stewart . . . I . . . look, it's rather difficult to talk through the door . . ."

But, before the word was out of his mouth, I had undone the snib, lifted the latch and opened it for him. And I did that apparently crazy thing because of the way he had said his own name. Stewart. Americans invariably find it difficult to pronounce . . . Stoowart, they call it. But he had said Stewart the way my grandmother said it, so he wasn't an American, he came from home. And, with a name like that, he probably came from Scotland.

I suppose I had imagined that I should immediately recognize him, but in fact I had never seen him before in my life. He stood before me, with the headlights of his car still bright behind him, and only firelight to show me his face. He wore horn-rimmed spectacles and he was tall . . . taller than I was. We stared at each other, he startled by my swift change of policy, and I suddenly engulfed by a great wave of pure fury. Nothing makes me so angry as being frightened, and I had been scared half crazy.

"What do you want to come sneaking up like that for, in the middle of the night . . ." even to myself my voice sounded shrill and not entirely in control.

He answered, reasonably enough, "It's only nine o'clock, and I didn't mean to sneak up."

"You could have phoned and let me know you were coming."

"I couldn't find any number in the book." He had made no move to come in. Rusty was still glowering away in the background. "And I had no idea you'd be on your own or I'd have waited."

My rage was subsiding, and I felt a little ashamed of my outburst. "Well . . . now you're here, you'd better come in." I backed off and reached for the switch. The room sprang into cold, bright, electric light.

But he still hesitated. "Don't you want any credentials . . . you know, credit card? Passport?"

I looked at him sharply, thought I detected a gleam of amusement behind the glasses, wondered what he found so damn funny. "If you'd lived out here as long as I have, you wouldn't open the door to any creepy prowler either."

"Well, before the creepy prowler comes in, perhaps he'd better go and turn off the car lights. I left them on so that I could see my way."

Without waiting for the snappy answer which I would have loved to be able to deliver, he went back outside. I left the door open and went back to the fire and put on another log, and found that my hands were shaking and my heart thumping like a drum. I straightened the hearth-rug, kicked Rusty's bone under the chair and was lighting myself a cigarette when he came back into the cabin, shutting the back porch door behind him.

I turned to face him. He was dark, with the pale skin and black hair that a good many Highlanders possess, thin and rather scholarly looking in an angular and uncoordinated way. He wore a smooth tweed suit, worn slightly at elbows and knees and buttonholes, a brown and white checked shirt, and a dark green tie, and he looked as though he might be a schoolmaster or a professor of some obscure science. There was no guessing at his age. He could have been anything between thirty and fifty.

He said, "How do you feel now?"

"I'm all right," but my hand was still shaking and he saw it.

"It wouldn't do you any harm to have a little drink."

"I don't know if there's anything in the house."

"Where could we look?"

"Under the window seat?"

He went over and opened the cupboard, groped around a bit, and came out with fluff all over the sleeve of his coat and a quarter of a bottle of Haig in his hand.

"The very thing. Now all we need is a glass."

I went into the kitchen and came back with two and a jug of water, and the ice-tray out of the refrigerator, and watched while he poured the drinks. They looked suspiciously dark. I said, "I don't like whisky, much."

"Think of it as medicine." He handed it to me.

"I don't want to get plastered."

"On that, you won't."

It made sense. The whisky tasted smoky and was marvellously warming. Comforted by it, embarrassed at having been such a ninny, I smiled tentatively at him.

He grinned back. "Why don't we sit down?"

So we sat, me on the hearthrug, and he on the edge of Father's big chair, his hands loose between his knees, and the drink on the floor between his feet. He said, "Out of interest, what made you suddenly open the door?"

"It was the way you said your name. Stewart. You come from Scotland, don't you?"

"Yes."

"Whereabouts?"

"Caple Bridge."

"But that's near Elvie."

"I know. You see, I'm with Ramsay McKenzie and King . . ."

"My grandmother's lawyers."

"That's right."

"But I don't remember you."

"I didn't join the firm until five years ago."

There was a coldness around my heart, but I made myself ask: "There's nothing . . . wrong?"

"Nothing wrong." His voice was very reassuring.

"Then why have you come?"

"It's a question," said David Stewart, "of a number of unanswered letters."

Chapter 3

AFTER A LITTLE I said, "I don't understand."

"Four, to be exact. Three from Mrs Bailey herself and one from me, written on her behalf."

"Written who to?" It was not a time to worry about my grammar.

"Your father."

"When?"

"During the course of the last two months."

"Did you send the letters here? I mean, we move around so much."

"You had written to your grandmother yourself, giving her this address."

This was true. I always let her know when we moved. I threw my half-smoked cigarette into the fire, and tried to get used to this extraordinary situation. My father, for all his faults, was a most un-secret man . . . if anything, he erred in the opposite direction, loudly fuming and complaining for days on end if anything annoyed or disturbed him. But I had heard nothing about any letters.

He prompted me. "You haven't seen any letters?"

"No. But that's not surprising because Father always collects the mail himself, every day, from the drug store."

"Perhaps he never opened them?"

But this, too, was out of character. Father always opened letters. He didn't necessarily read them, but there was always the happy possibility that the envelope might contain a cheque.

I said, "No, he wouldn't do that." I swallowed the nervous lump in my throat and pushed my hair back off my face. "What were they about? Or perhaps you don't know."

"Yes, of course I know." He could sound very dry, and it wasn't difficult to imagine him ensconced behind an old-fashioned desk, clearing his throat along with his emotions, and dealing crisply with all the incomprehensible pitfalls of wills, affidavits, sales, leases and orders to view. "It's just that your grandmother wants you to come back to Scotland . . . pay a visit . . ."

I said, "I know she does—she's always talking about it in her letters."

He raised an eyebrow. "Don't you want to come?"

"Yes . . . of course I do . . ."

I thought of Father, remembered that long-ago overheard conversation. "I don't know . . . I mean, I can't just make up my mind like that. . . ."

"Is there any reason why you shouldn't come?"

"Well, of course there is . . . my father . . ."

"You mean, there's no one to keep house for him?"

"No I don't mean that at all." He waited for me to enlarge on this statement, perhaps to tell him what I did mean. I didn't want to meet his eye, and turned away from him to stare into the fire. I had an uncomfortable suspicion that my face wore an expression which could be described as sheepish.

He said, "You know, there was never any bad feeling about the fact that your father brought you over to America . . ."

"She wanted me to stay at Elvie."

"You know that, then?"

"Yes, I heard them quarrelling. They never quarrelled usually. I think they got on very well. But there was a terrible row over me."

"But that was seven years ago. Now, surely, between us, we can make some arrangements."

I made the most obvious excuse. "But it's so expensive . . ."

"Mrs Bailey, of course, will stand you the fare." (I imagined, ruefully, Father's reaction to this.) "You don't need to be away for more than a month." He said again, "Don't you want to come?"

His manner disarmed me. "Yes, of course I do . . ."

"Then why this lack of enthusiasm?"

"I don't want to upset my father. And he obviously doesn't want me to come, or he'd have answered those letters you spoke about."

"Yes, the letters. I wonder where they would be."

I indicated the table behind him, the pile of manuscript and reference books, old files, envelopes and regrettably unpaid bills. "Over there, I suppose."

"I wonder why he never told you about them."

I said nothing, but thought that I knew. In a way, he resented Elvie and the fact that it meant so much to me. He was, perhaps, a little jealous of my mother's family. He was afraid of losing me.

I said, "I've no idea."

"Well, when are you expecting him back from Los Angeles?"

I said, "I don't think you should see him. It would only make him miserable, because even if he agreed to my going, I couldn't leave him alone, here."

"But surely we could arrange something . . ."

"No, we couldn't. He has to have someone to look after him. He's the most impractical person in the world . . . he'd never buy any food, or gas for the car, and if I left him, I'd just be worried sick about him all the time."

"Jane . . . you do have to think about yourself. . . ."

"Some other time I'll come. Tell my grandmother some other time."

In silence he considered this. He finished his drink, and then set down the empty glass. "Well, let's leave it like this. I'm driving back to Los Angeles tomorrow morning, about eleven. I have a seat booked for you on the plane to New York, Tuesday morning. There's no reason on earth why you shouldn't sleep on this, and if you change your mind . . ."

"I won't."

He ignored this. "If you change your mind, there's nothing to stop you coming with me." He stood up, looming over me. "And I still think that you should."

I don't like being loomed over, so I stood up too.

"You seemed very sure that I would come with you."

"I hoped that you would."

"You think I'm just making excuses, don't you?"

"Not entirely."

"I feel very guilty that you've travelled so far for nothing."

"I was in New York, on business. And I've enjoyed meeting you, and only sorry that I missed your father." He held out his hand. "Goodbye, Jane." After a second's hesitation, I put mine into it. Americans aren't much good at shaking hands and one gets out of the habit. "And I'll send your love to your grandmother."

"Yes, and Sinclair."

"Sinclair?"

"You see him, don't you? When he comes to Elvie?"

"Yes. Yes, of course I do. And I'll certainly give him your love."

I said, "Tell him to write," and then bent to make a fuss of Rusty, because my eyes were filled with tears, and I didn't want David Stewart to see.

When he had gone, I went back into the cabin, and over to the table where my father kept all his papers. After a little I found, one by one, the four unanswered letters, all opened, and obviously read. I didn't read them. My finer instincts prevailed—and anyway I already knew what they contained, so I simply replaced them, buried as before.

I went to kneel on the window seat, to open the window and hang out. It was very dark, the ocean inky, the air cold, but my terrors had evaporated. I thought of Elvie, and longed to be there. I thought of geese flying the winter skies, and the smell of peat burning in the fireplace in the hall. I thought of the loch, brilliant blue and calm as a mirror, or grey and lashed into white waves by northern gales. I wanted to be there, suddenly, so badly that it was a physical ache.

And I was angry with my father. I didn't want to leave him, but surely he could have discussed the matter with me, given me the chance to make my own decision. I was twenty-one, no longer a child, and resented what I considered an unbearingly selfish and old-fashioned attitude.

Just wait till he gets back, I promised myself. *Wait till I face him with those letters. I'll just tell him . . . I'll . . .*

But my anger was short-lived. I could never stay angry for long. Cooled by the night air, perhaps, it simmered away and died, and I was left, feeling strangely flat. Nothing, after all, had changed. I would stay with him because I loved him, because he wanted me, because he needed me. There was no possible alternative. And I would not confront him with the letters, because to be found out would embarrass and demean him, and it was important, if we were to have any sort of a future together, that he would always be bigger and stronger and wiser than I was.

I was engaged in scrubbing the kitchen floor the next morning, when I heard the unmistakable grinding of the old Dodge as it came over the hill and down the track to Reef Point. I hastily swiped at the last square foot or so of cracked brown linoleum, then got up off my knees, wrang out the floor cloth, emptied the dirty water down the drain, and went out through the back porch door to meet my father, wiping my hands on the old striped apron as I went.

It was a gorgeous day; the sun hot, the sky blue and scudding with bright white clouds, the sparkling morning filled with wind and the crash of high-tide rollers pouring up on to the beach. I had already done a line of washing and now it strained and flapped at the rope, and I ducked beneath this and went out on to the road as the car came bumping and lurching over the ruts towards me.

I saw at once that my father was not alone. Because of the fine weather, he had put the hood down, and beside him, unmistakable head of red hair a-blow in the breeze, sat Linda Lansing. When she saw me she hung over the side of the car to wave, and her white poodle, sitting on her knee, hung out too, and went into a paroxysm of barking as though I had no right to be there.

Rusty, who had been out on the beach having a good game with an old bit of basket, heard the poodle, and came at once to my rescue, galloping around the corner of the cabin in full cry, snarling and barking, and making little dashes at the Dodge with his teeth bared, unable to wait for the happy moment when he could sink them into the poodle's neck. My father swore, Linda screamed and hugged the poodle, the poodle yapped, and I had to take Rusty by his flea collar and haul him indoors and order him to shut up and behave, before there was the slightest chance of any sort of human conversation.

I left Rusty sulking and went back out again. My father was out of the car. "Hello, cutie." He came around to give me a hug and a kiss. It was like being hugged by a gorilla and his beard scraped my cheek. "Everything all right?"

"Yes, fine," I turned from his embrace. "Hi Linda."

"Hi, honey."

"Sorry about the dog." I went to open the door for her. She wore full make-up, false eyelashes, a pale blue jump suit and gold ballet slippers. The poodle had a pink collar, studded with rhinestones.

"That's OK. Mitzi's highly-strung I guess. Something to do with being so highly-bred." She put up her face, lips bunched, to receive my kiss. I gave her one and the poodle started yapping again.

"For God's sake," said my father, "keep that bloody dog quiet," whereupon Linda tipped it unceremoniously out of the car and climbed out after it.

Linda Lansing was an actress. Twenty years or so ago she had turned up in Hollywood as a starlet, which meant a prodigious per-

sonal publicity campaign followed by a string of undistinguished mov-
ies, in which she usually played some sort of a gypsy or peasant girl,
wearing an off-the-shoulder drawnstring blouse, dark red lips and
brooding expression, very sulky. But, inevitably, this type of movie,
along with her style of acting, went out of fashion, and Linda went
with them. Astutely, for she was never stupid, she swiftly married. "My
husband comes before my career," read the captions beneath their
wedding photographs, and for some time she disappeared from the
Hollywood scene altogether. But lately, having divorced her third husband, and not yet having buttonholed the fourth, she had started to
appear again, in small parts and on television. To a young generation of
viewers, she was a new face, and, with clever direction, revealed an
entirely unsuspected flair for comedy.

We had met her at one of those dreary Sunday brunch pool parties which were so much part of the Los Angeles scene. My father had
latched on to her at once, as being the only woman in the place worth
talking to. I like her as well. She has a vulgar sense of humour, a deep
plummy voice and a surprising ability to laugh at herself.

My father is attractive to women, but has always handled his liai-
sons with an admirable discretion. I knew that he had embarked on an
affair with Linda, but I had hardly expected that he would bring her
back to Reef Point with him.

I decided to play it very cool. "Well, this is a surprise. What are
you doing in this neck of the woods?"

"Oh, you know how it is, honey, when your father starts twisting
your arm. And just smell that sea air." She took a great lungful,
coughed slightly, and turned back to the car to extricate her handbag.
It was then that I saw the lavish luggage piled on the back seat. Three
cases, a wardrobe-bag, a beauty box, a mink coat in a plastic bag, and
Mitzi's dog basket, complete with pink rubber bone. I gaped at its
quantity, but before I could say anything, my father had elbowed me
out of the way and already lifted out two of the cases.

"Well, don't stand there with your mouth open," he said. "Bring
something in."

And with that he headed for the cabin. Linda, after one look at my
expression, tactfully decided that Mitzi needed a run on the beach and
disappeared. I started after my father, and then thought better of it,
went back for the dog basket, and started off again.

I found him in the living-room having put the two suitcases down
in the middle of the floor, thrown his long-peaked cap on to a chair,

and unloaded some bundles of old letters and papers out of his pocket on to the table. The room, which I had only just cleaned and tidied, became immediately disordered, impermanent, frantic. My father could do this to any place simply by walking into it. Now, he went over to the window to lean out and check on the view, and get a good lungful of sea air. Over his massive shoulder I could see the distant figure of Linda, skittering about with the poodle at the sea's edge. Rusty, still sulking on the window seat, did not even thump his tail.

My father turned, reaching in his shirt pocket for his cigarettes. He appeared delighted with himself. "Well," he said, "aren't you going to ask how everything went?" He lit the cigarette, and then looked up, and frowned, flicking the lighted match out of the window behind him. "What are you standing holding the dog basket for? Put the bloody thing down."

I didn't. I said, "What's going on?"

"What do you mean?"

I realized that all this hearty good cheer was part of a big bluster.

"You know very well what I mean. Linda."

"What about Linda? You like her, don't you?"

"Of course I like her, but that's hardly the point. What's she doing here?"

"I've asked her to stay."

"With all that luggage? "How long for, for heaven's sake?"

"Well . . ." he gestured vaguely with his hand. "For as long as she wants."

"Isn't she working?"

"Oh, she's chucked all that." He went prowling off to the kitchen in search of a can of beer. I heard the refrigerator opening and shutting. "She gets just about as sick of L.A. as we did. So I thought why not?" He appeared again at the open kitchen door with the open beer can in his hand. "The suggestion was hardly out of my mouth, when she found someone to rent her house, along with the maid, and she was packed and ready." He frowned again. "Jane, have you conceived some sort of an affection for that dog basket?"

I continued to ignore him. "For how long?" I insisted grimly.

"Well, as long as we do. I don't know. For the winter maybe."

I said, "There isn't room."

"Of course there's room. And whose house is this anyway?" He drained the beer can, tossed it neatly across the kitchen into the trash can, and went out to bring in the next load of luggage. This time he carried the cases into his bedroom. I put down Mitzi's dog basket and followed him. What with the bed and the suitcases and the two of us, there wasn't much room.

I said, "Where's she going to sleep?"

"Well, where do you think she's going to sleep?" He sat on the monstrous bed, and the springs complained bitterly. "Right here."

I could think of nothing to say. I simply stared at him. This had never, ever happened before. I wondered if he had gone out of his mind.

Something in my face must have got through to him then, for he suddenly looked contrite and took my hands.

"Janey, don't look like that. You're not a kid any more, I don't have to pretend to you. You like Linda, I wouldn't have brought her back if I didn't know you liked her. And she'll be company for you, I won't have to leave you alone so much. Oh, come on, take that dismal face off and go and make a pot of coffee."

I pulled my hands free. I said, "I haven't got time."

"What do you mean?"

"I . . . I have to go and pack."

I went out of his room, and into my own, and I pulled my suitcase out from under the bed, and put it on the bed and opened it, and started to pack, like people do in films, opening drawers one by one and emptying them into the suitcase.

From the open door behind me my father spoke.

"What do you think you're doing?"

I turned to look at him, my hands full of shirts and belts and scarves and handkerchiefs. I said, "I'm going."

"Where?"

"Back to Scotland."

He took a single step into the room, and jerked me round to face him. I went on quickly, not letting him say a word. "You had four letters," I told him. "Three from my grandmother and one from the solicitors. You opened them and you read them and you never told me, because you didn't want me to go back. You didn't even discuss them with me."

His grip on my arm never loosened, but I thought his face lost a little of its colour.

"How did you know about those letters?"

I told him about David Stewart. "He told me everything," I finished. "Not that I needed to be told," I added recklessly, "because I knew it all anyway."

"And just what exactly did you know?"

"That you never wanted me to stay at Elvie after Mother died. That you wouldn't ever want me to go back." He watched me, puzzled. "I was *listening*," I shouted at him, as though he had suddenly gone deaf. "I was in the hall, listening, and I heard everything that you and my grandmother said to each other."

"And you never said a word?"

"What good would it have done?"

He sat carefully on the edge of my bed, so as not to disturb my packing. "Did you want to be left behind?"

His obtuseness infuriated me. "No, of course I didn't, I've loved being with you, I wouldn't have had it any other way, but that was all seven years ago, and now I'm an adult, and you had no right to hide away those letters and not say anything to me."

"Do you want to go back so badly?"

"Yes, I do. I love Elvie, you know how much it means to me." I picked up a hairbrush, my photographs, jammed them down the sides of the case. "I . . . I wasn't going to say anything about the letters. I thought it would make you miserable, and I couldn't go anyway, because you hadn't anyone to look after you. But now, it's different."

"All right, so it's different, and you're going. I'm not going to stop you. But how are you going to get there?"

"David Stewart's leaving La Carmella at eleven. If I hurry I can catch him. He has a seat booked for me on the New York plane tomorrow morning."

"And when are you coming back?"

"Oh, I don't know. Some time I suppose." I pushed in a book, Anne Morrow Lindbergh's *Gift from the Sea*, which I can never be without, and my Simon and Garfunkel LP. I shut down the lid of the case, and everything bulged out and it wouldn't close, so I opened it again, and flattened things frantically, and still it wouldn't work, and in the end it was my father who did it for me, by sheer brute force, holding down the lid of the case, and forcing the locks to snib.

Over the closed suitcase, I met his eye. I said, "I wouldn't be going if Linda hadn't come . . ." My voice trailed away. I took my raincoat from the hook on the back of the door, and put it on over my shirt and jeans.

My father said, "You're still wearing your apron."

It was the sort of thing that once we would have laughed at. Now, in deathly silence I reached round and untied it, and tore it off, and dropped it across the bed.

I said, "If I take the car, and leave it at the motel, could you or Linda pick it up?"

"Sure," said my father . . . and then, "Wait . . ." and he disappeared into his room again, only to return with a fist full of money, five dollar bills, ten dollars, one dollar, all dirty and ragged as a bundle of old newspapers. "Here," he said, and shoved them into the pocket of my raincoat, "you'd better take this. You might need it."

I said, "But you . . ." but at that moment Linda and Mitzi chose to return from the beach, Mitzi shedding sand all over the floor, and Linda delighted with her short commune with nature.

"Oh, those waves, I've never seen anything like them. They must be ten feet high." She noticed then, my suitcase, my raincoat, my presumably miserable face. "Jane, what are you doing?"

"I'm going away."

"Where, for heaven's sakes?"

"To Scotland."

"I hope not because of me."

"Partly. But only because it means that there's someone to look after Father."

She looked a little disconcerted, as though looking after Father had been the last thing she expected to do, but she gamely covered up and made the best of it. "Well, that's fun for you. When're you going?"

"Today. Now. I'm taking the Dodge over to La Carmella . . ." I had already started to back away, because the situation was becoming more than I could bear. My father picked up my case and came after me. "And I hope you have a good winter. And that there aren't too many storms. And there are eggs and canned tuna fish in the icebox . . ."

I went backwards down the porch steps, was out of the house, turned, and ducked under the line of washing (would Linda have the sense to bring it in?), and I got in behind the wheel of the car and my father heaved the suitcase in on to the back seat.

"Jane—" but I was incapable of saying goodbye. I was actually moving, on my way, when I remembered Rusty. By then it was too late. He had heard me, heard the car door, heard the engine start up, and he was out of the house and after me like a shot, barking indignantly, racing alongside me, his ears flat against his head, and in imminent danger of almost certain death.

It was the last straw. I stopped the car. My father with a great bellow of "Rusty!" came after the dog. Rusty stood on his back legs and scratched and scrabbled with his claws on the car door, and I leaned over and tried to push him off and said, "Oh, Rusty, don't. Get down. I can't take you. I can't take you with me."

Father, actually running, had caught up with us. He swept Rusty up into his arms and stood looking down at me. Rusty's eyes were hurt and reproachful, but my father had an expression in his face which I had never seen before and did not wholly understand. But I knew in that moment I didn't want to say goodbye to either of them, and I burst into tears.

"You will look after Rusty, won't you?" I bawled, my mouth going square. "Shut him up so that he can't follow the car. And don't let him get run over. And he only likes Red Heart dog food, not the other kind. And don't leave him alone on the beach, someone might steal him." I groped for a handkerchief. As usual I hadn't got one, and as usual, my father took one out of his pocket, and silently handed it to me. I blew my nose, and then I put up my arms, and pulled him down so that I could kiss him, and Rusty too, and I said goodbye and Father said, "Goodbye, my Pooch," which he hasn't called me since I was six, and bawling harder than ever, and hardly able to see a thing, I never looked back, but I knew that they stood there, and that they watched until I was over the ridge and out of sight.

It was a quarter to eleven when I walked into the reception office of the motel and the man behind the desk looked at my blurred and tear-stained face without interest, as though weeping females came in and out all day long.

I said, "Has Mr David Stewart left yet?"

"No, he's still around. Got a phone bill to settle up."

"What number's his room?"

He glanced at a board. "Thirty-two." His eyes ran over my raincoat, my jeans, my stained sneakers, and his hand reached for the phone. "You want to see him?"

"Yes, please."

"I'll call him . . . tell him you're coming. What's your name?"

"Jane Marsh."

He ducked his head in the direction of the door, sending me on my way. "Number thirty-two," he said.

30

I set off blindly, down a covered path which led alongside a large, very blue swimming pool. Two women lay in long chairs and their children swam and screamed and fought over a rubber ring. Before I had got halfway, David Stewart was coming to meet me. When I saw him I started to run, and much to the interest of the two women, and also to my own surprise, I ran straight into his arms, and he caught me and gave me a reassuring sort of hug, and then held me off and said, "What's wrong?"

"Nothing's wrong." But I had started to cry again. "I'm coming with you."

"Why?"

"I've changed my mind, that's all."

"Why?"

I hadn't meant to tell him, but it all started spilling out. "Father's got a friend, and she's come from Los Angeles . . . and she's . . . she said . . ."

He took a look at the two goggling women, said, "Come along," and led me back to the privacy of his room, pushed me inside, and shut the door behind us.

"Now," he said.

I blew my nose and made a real effort to pull myself together.

"It's just that he has someone to look after him. So I can come with you."

"Did you tell him about the letters?"

"Yes."

"And doesn't he mind your coming?"

"No. He said O.K."

David was quiet. I looked at him and saw that he had turned his head, was now regarding me thoughtfully from the corner of his right eye. I found out later that this was a habit picked up over the years on account of his bad eyesight and the fact that he had to wear glasses, but at the moment it was both disconcerting and uncomfortable; like being nailed to the wall.

I said miserably, "Don't you want me to come with you?"

"It's not that. It's just that I don't know you well enough to know if you're telling the truth."

I was too unhappy to be offended. "I never lie," I said, and then amended this. "And when I do I go all shifty and blush. And Father did say it was all right." And to prove this I put my hand in my raincoat pocket and pulled out the dirty bundle of dollars. Some of the bills fell, like old leaves, to the carpet. "He gave me some money to spend."

David stooped and picked them up and handed them back to me. "I still think, Jane, I should make a point of seeing him before we fly off. We could . . ."

"I couldn't say goodbye again."

His face lost its severity. He touched my arm. "Stay here then. I won't be more than fifteen minutes."

"You promise?"

"I promise."

He went, and I wandered around the room he had occupied, and read a bit of a newspaper, and looked out of the open door, and then went into the bathroom and washed my face and my hands, and combed my hair and found a rubber band and fastened it back. I went out and sat by the pool and waited for him, and when he returned and had loaded our luggage, I got into the car beside him, and we drove out and on to the highway and south to Los Angeles. We stayed the night in a motel near the airport, and the next day we flew to New York, and the next night, to London, and it was not until we were halfway out over the Atlantic that I remembered the young boy who had been coming, next Sunday, to take me surfing.

Chapter 4

I HAD LIVED for most of my life in London, but returning was like coming to a city I had never seen before, so changed was it. The airport buildings, the approach roads, the skyline, the great towering blocks of flats, the mass of traffic . . . all this had happened in the last seven years. In the taxi I sat wedged in a corner with my case at my feet, and it was foggy so that the street lights still burned, and damply cold in a way that I had forgotten.

I had not slept in the plane and was dizzy with fatigue; nauseated by unlikely meals presented to me at what was, according to my watch, which I had kept at California time, two o'clock in the morning. My body, my head, my eyes ached with travelling, my teeth felt gritty, and my clothes as though I had been wearing them forever.

There were billboards, fly-overs, rows of houses, and London enclosed us. The taxi turned off at some traffic lights, nosed its way down a quiet crescent, lined with parked cars, and stopped in front of a terrace of tall, early Victorian houses.

I watched them dully and wondered what I was meant to do now. David leaned across me and opened the door and said, "This is where we get out."

"Uh?" I looked at him and wondered how any man, who had shared the—to me—soul-destroying experience of flying, non-stop, half-way round the world, could continue to look clean, relaxed and in charge of the situation. But I fell obediently out of the taxi and stood on the pavement, blinking like an owl and yawning, while he paid the driver off, collected our suitcases, and led the way down a flight of basement steps. The railings which enclosed them were shiny black, the little paved area was clean and swept, and there was a wooden tub full of geraniums . . . a little sooty, but still bright and gay. He took out a key, the yellow door swung inwards, and I followed him blindly into the flat.

It was white-painted, smelt of country houses, the floor was scattered with Persian rugs, there were chintz covers on the sofa and armchairs, small, old, polished pieces of furniture, a Venetian mirror over the fireplace. I saw books and a pile of magazines, a glass-fronted cabinet filled with Dresden, small patches of hand-worked tapestry . . . and, beyond the windows on the far side of the room, a miniature sunken patio garden, with a plane tree, ringed by a wooden seat, and a small statue set into the recess of the faded brick wall.

I stood, yawning. He went to open a window, and I said, "Is this your flat?"

"No, it's my mother's, but I use it when I come to London."

I looked around vaguely. "Where is your mother?" It sounded as though I expected her to be hiding under the sofa, but he didn't smile.

"She's in the South of France, on holiday. Come on now, take off your coat, and get comfortable. I'll go and make a cup of tea."

He disappeared through a door. I heard the sound of a tap turned on, a kettle being filled. A cup of tea. The very words were comforting and homely. A cup of tea. I thought of elocution lessons. How Now Brown Cow How Would You Like A Cup Of Tea. I fumbled with the buttons of my raincoat, and eventually got them undone, pulled the coat off and draped it across what looked like a Chippendale chair. I let myself down on to the sofa. It had leaf green velvet cushions and I took one and pulled it into position and put my head down, but I think I was asleep before I actually had time to get my feet up off the floor. I certainly don't remember doing this.

When I awoke, the light had changed. A long beam of sunshine, dancing with dust, lay like a spotlight across my line of vision. I moved, and knuckled the sleep from my eyes, and looked again, and there was a rug over me, warm and light.

In the fireplace, a fire flickered. I looked at it for some time before I realized that it was an electric one with sham logs and coal and flames. It seemed, at that moment, infinitely cosy. I turned my head slightly and saw David, deep in an arm-chair, a-wash in papers and brief-cases. He had on different clothes—a blue shirt, a cream-coloured sweater with a V-neck. I wondered in a detached sort of way if he was one of those people who never needed to sleep. He had heard my stirrings and was watching me.

I said, "What day is it?"

He was amused. "Wednesday."

"Where are we?"

"London."

"No. I mean, whereabouts?"

"Kensington."

I said, "We used to live in Melbury Road. Is that far?"

"No. Quite near."

After a little. "What time is it?"

"Nearly five."

"When do we go to Scotland?"

"Tonight. We've got sleepers booked on the Royal Highlander."

With an enormous effort I sat up, and yawned and tried to wipe sleep out of my system and hair out of my face. I said, "I suppose I couldn't possibly have a bath?"

"Of course you can," he said.

So I had a bath, boiling water that wouldn't lather properly and handfuls of his mother's bath salts which he kindly said I could use. When I had bathed I got my suitcase, and found some clean clothes and put them on, and jammed all the dirty ones back in the case, and somehow got the case shut again, and went back into the sitting-room, and found that he had made tea, and that there was hot buttered toast and a plate of chocolate biscuits—the proper kind, not chocolate flavoured cookies which you get in America, but plain biscuits covered with real chocolate.

I said, "Are these your mother's?"

"No. I went out and bought them while you were asleep. There's a little shop around the corner, very handy when you run out of things."

"Has your mother lived here always?"

"Not at all, only a year or so. She used to have a house in Hampshire, but it got too big for her and the garden was a worry . . . it's not easy to get help. So she sold it, and kept a few of her favourite things and moved here."

So that explained the country house atmosphere. I looked out at the little patio and said, "And she has got a garden."

"Yes, a small one. But she can manage that herself."

I took another piece of toast and tried to imagine my grandmother in such a situation. But it was not possible. Grandmother would never be defeated by the size of her house or the amount she had to do, or the difficulties of getting and keeping cooks and gardeners. Indeed, Mrs Lumley had been with her ever since I could remember, standing on her swollen legs at the kitchen table, and rolling out pastry. And Will, the gardener, had a little cottage and an allotment of his own, where he grew potatoes and carrots and enormous mop-headed chrysanthemums.

"So you didn't ever live in this flat?"

"No, but I stay with her when I come to London."

"Is that often?"

"Fairly."

"Do you ever see Sinclair?"

"Yes."

"What does he do?"

"He works for an advertising agency. I would have thought you knew that."

It occurred to me that I could ring him up. After all, he lived in London, it would take only moments to look up his number. I thought of doing this, and then decided against it. I was not entirely sure of Sinclair's reaction, and did not wish David Stewart to witness my possible discomfiture.

I said, "Has he got a girl-friend?"

"Heaps, I should think."

"No, you know what I mean. Anyone very special."

"Jane, I really wouldn't know."

I licked hot butter, thoughtfully, from the ends of my fingers. I said, "Do you suppose he'll come up to Elvie when I'm there?"

"Bound to."

"And his father? Is Uncle Aylwyn still in Canada?"

David Stewart pushed his glasses up his nose with a long, brown finger. He said, "Aylwyn Bailey died, about three months ago."

I stared. "Now I never knew *that*. Oh, poor Granny. Was she very upset?"

"Yes, she was . . ."

"And the funeral and everything . . ."

"In Canada. He'd been ill for some time. He never managed to get home."

"So Sinclair never saw him again."

"No."

I digested this information, and felt sad. I thought of my own father, infuriating as he was, and knew that not for anything would I have missed a single moment of the time we had spent together, and I felt sadder than ever for Sinclair. And then I remembered that in the old days it had been I who envied him, for, while I merely spent holidays at Elvie, it was Sinclair's home. And as for missing a father's companionship, the place had always been teeming with men, for as well as Will the gardener—whom we loved—there was Gibson the keeper, a dour man but wise in all respects; and Gibson's two sons, Hamish and George, who were about Sinclair's age and included him in all their pursuits, both legal and otherwise. And so he had been taught to shoot and cast a fly, play cricket and climb trees, and one way and another had a good deal more time and attention lavished on him than most boys of his age. No, all things considered, Sinclair had missed very little.

We caught the Royal Highlander at Euston, and it seemed that I spent half the night getting out of bed to look out of the window and gloat over the fact that the train was tearing northwards, and nothing, save a disastrous Act of God, could stop it. In Edinburgh I was wakened by a female voice, sounding like Maggie Smith being Miss Jean Brodie, saying "Edinburgh Waverley. This is Edinburgh Waverley," and I knew that I was in Scotland, and I got up and put my raincoat over my nightdress and sat on the cover of the wash basin and watched as the lights of Edinburgh slid away, and waited for the bridge, when the train, suddenly making an entirely different sound, plunged out and over the Forth, and the river lay miles below us, a gleam of dark water, touched with the riding lights of miniature craft.

I got back into bed, and dozed until we reached Relkirk, when I got up again, and opened the window, and the air poured in, cold and edged with the smell of peat and pine. We were on the edge of the Highlands. It was only a quarter past five, but I dressed and spent the last part of the journey with my cheek pressed against the dark, rain-spattered glass. To begin with I could see little, but by the time we had ground our way over the pass, and started in on the long run down the gentle gradient that finally leads to Thrumbo, the day was beginning to lighten. There was no sign of the sun, simply an imperceptible fading from darkness. Clouds were thick, grey and soft over the tops of the hills, but as we ran down into the valley, they thinned and shredded away to nothing and the great wide sweep of the glen lay before us, golden brown and tranquil in the early morning light.

There was a thump on my door and the attendant looked in.

"The gentleman's wanting to know if you're awake. We'll be in to Thrumbo in ten minutes or so. Will I take your case?"

He removed it, and the door shut behind him and I turned back to the window, because now the countryside was becoming closely familiar and I didn't want to miss a thing. I had walked on that bit of road, ridden a highland pony in that field, had been taken to tea in that white cottage. And then there was the bridge which marked the boundaries of the village, and the filling station, and the refined hotel that was always filled with elderly residents, and where you could never buy a drink.

The door opened again, and David Stewart stood there, filling the doorway.

"Good morning."

"Hi."

"How did you sleep?"

"O.K."

Now the train was slowing, braking. We moved past the signal box, under the bridge. I slid off the top of the wash basin, and followed him out into the corridor, and over his shoulder watched the sign saying Thrumbo sail triumphantly past, and then the train stopped and we were there.

He had left his car in a garage, so he abandoned me to wait in the station yard while he went to fetch it. I sat there on my suitcase, in the deserted, slowly waking village, and watched as lights came on, one by one, and chimneys smoked, and a man came wobbling down the street on a bicycle. And then I heard, far above me, a honking and a chattering and it became louder and passed clear overhead but I couldn't see the formations of wild geese, because they were flying above the cloud.

Elvie Loch lay about two miles beyond the village of Thrumbo, a wild expanse of water looped to the north by the main road to Inverness and enclosed, on the opposite shore, by the great bastions of the Cairngorms. Elvie itself was very nearly an island, shaped like a mushroom and joined to the mainland by its stalk, a narrow spit of land that was no more than a causeway between reed-filled marshes, nesting-place for hundreds of birds.

For many years the land had belonged to the church, and indeed there were still the ruins of a little chapel, roofless now and deserted, although the small graveyard surrounding it was still kept neat and tidy, the yews tightly clipped, the grass mown smooth as velvet, and, in spring, gay with the tossing heads of wild daffodils.

The house where my grandmother lived had been the manse for this little church. Over the years, however, it had outstripped its original modest bounds, as wings were added and extra rooms to accommodate, one supposed, large Victorian families. From the back, from the approach road, it appeared tall and forbidding, the windows to the north being small and sparse in order to conserve warmth in the bitter winters, and the front door was snug and unimpressive, and usually tightly closed. This fortress-like impression was enhanced by the two high garden walls, which, like arms, reached from the house to east and west, and against which even my grandmother had been unable to coax a climber to grow.

But, from the other side, the aspect of Elvie was entirely different. The old white house, protected and enclosed and facing due south, blinked and drowsed in the sunlight. Windows and doors stood open to the fresh air, and the garden sloped down to a shallow ha-ha, dividing it from a narrow field where a neighbouring farmer grazed his cattle. The field dipped to the water's edge, and the lap of small waves on shingle, and the gentle lowing and munching of cattle were so constant a part of Elvie that after a little you stopped hearing them. It was only when you'd been away, and returned, that you became aware of them all over again.

David Stewart's car was a surprise, a dark blue T.R.4, and unexpectedly racy for such a solid-seeming citizen. We packed in our cases, and headed out of Thrumbo, and I sat forward on my seat and churned with excitement. Familiar landmarks appeared, and flew away behind us. The garage, the sweet shop, and the McGregors' farm, and then we were out in open country. The road swept up through fields of golden stubble, the hedges were spattered scarlet with the hips of wild roses, and there had been frost already, for trees were touched with the gold and red of the first autumn colours.

And then we swung around the last corner and the loch stretched away to our right, grey in the grey morning, and the mountains on the far side were lost in cloud. And, not half a mile away, stood Elvie itself, the house hidden by trees and the roofless church looking romantically desolate. Excitement made me speechless and, with a rare understanding, David Stewart offered no sort of comment. We had come a long way together, so far indeed that it was hard to comprehend, but it was in silence that we finally turned off by the roadside cottage, and the car wound down through the high hedges, over the causeway between the marshes, and up under the copper beeches, to come to a halt at the front door.

I was out of the car in an instant, running across the gravel, but my grandmother was quicker than I. The door opened and she appeared, and we met, our arms tight around each other, and she kept saying my name, and she smelt of the scented sachets she keeps with her clothes, and I told myself that nothing had changed.

Chapter 5

A REUNION after so many years is always confusion. We said things like, "Oh, you're really here . . ." and "I never thought I'd make it . . ." and "Did you have a good journey . . ." and "Everything's just the same," and we held each other off, and laughed at our idiocies, and hugged again.

Next the dogs added to the turmoil, boiling out of the house, barking around our feet, demanding attention. They were liver-and-white spaniels, new to me, and yet familiar too, because there had always been liver-and-white spaniels at Elvie, and these were no doubt descended from the ones I remembered. And no sooner had I started to greet the dogs than we were joined by Mrs Lumley, who had heard the din and was unable to resist the temptation to be in on the home-coming. She was fatter than ever in her green overall, and she appeared out of the house smiling from ear to ear, to be kissed, to tell me I'd grown awful tall and that I'd got more freckles than ever and that she was making a really big breakfast.

Behind me David was quietly unloading my suitcase, and now my grandmother went to greet him.

"David, you must be tired out." Rather to my surprise she gave him a kiss. "Thank you for bringing her safely back."

"You got my wire."

"Of course I did. I've been up since seven. You'll come in and have breakfast with us, won't you? We're expecting you."

But he excused himself, saying that his housekeeper would be expecting him, that he must get home and change and then get to the office.

"Well, then, come back for dinner tonight. Yes, I insist. About half past seven. We want to hear all about everything."

He allowed himself to be persuaded, and we looked at each other, smiling. It occurred to me, with some surprise, that I had only met him four days ago, and yet now, when it was time to say goodbye, I felt that I was leaving an old friend, someone I had known all my life. He had been given a difficult job to do, and he had done it tactfully and with good humour, and as far as I knew, had offended nobody.

"Oh, David . . ."

He hastily forestalled my garbled thanks.

"I'll see you this evening, Jane," and he backed away, and got into his car, and slammed the door, and we watched him turn and drive away, under the beeches, down the road and so around the corner and out of sight.

"Such a nice man," said my grandmother thoughtfully. "Don't you think so?"

"Yes," I said, "sweet," and dived to prevent Mrs Lumley picking up my case, and carried it into the house myself, and Grandmother and the dogs came behind me, and the door was shut and David Stewart was, for the moment, forgotten.

I was assailed by the smell of peat smoke from the hall fire, the smell of roses from the big bowl of pink blooms on the chest by the clock. One of the dogs was panting for attention, tail wagging and all excitement, and I stopped to scratch his ears and was just going to tell them about Rusty, when my grandmother said, "I've got a surprise for you, Jane," and I straightened and looked up and saw a man coming down the stairs towards me, silhouetted against the light of the staircase window. For an instant I was dazzled by this light, and then he said, "Hello Jane," and I realized that it was my cousin Sinclair.

I could only gape, while Grandmother and Mrs Lumley stood, delighted by the success of the surprise they had planned. He had reached my side, and taken my shoulders between his hands and stopped to kiss me before I found breath to say weakly, "But I thought you were in London."

"Well I'm not. I'm here."

"But how . . . ? Why . . . ?"

"I've got a few days' leave."

For me? Had he taken them so that he could be at Elvie for my return? The possibility was both flattering and exciting, but before I could say anything more, my grandmother started organizing us.

"Well, there's no point in our standing around here . . . Sinclair, perhaps you'd carry Jane's case up to her room, and then when you've washed your hands, dear, you'd better come down and have some breakfast. You'll be tired out after that journey."

"I'm not tired." And indeed I wasn't. I felt vital and wide awake and ready for anything. Sinclair picked up my case, and went upstairs two at a time, and I followed his long legs as though I had wings on my heels.

My bedroom, looking out over the garden and the loch, was inhumanly neat and polished but otherwise unchanged. Still, the white-painted bed stood, pushed in the bay of the window which was where I always preferred to sleep. And there was a pin cushion on the dressing-table and lavender bags in the wardrobe and the blue rug, covering the worn patch of carpet.

While I shed my coat and washed my hands, Sinclair went and dumped himself on my bed, sadly creasing the starched white cover, and watched me. In the seven years that had passed he had changed, of course, but the differences I saw in him were almost too subtle to be pin-pointed. He was thinner, certainly, there were fine lines round his mouth and at the corners of his eyes, but that was all. He was very good looking, with dark brows and lashes and deep blue eyes, which slanted tantalizingly up at the corners. His nose was straight and his mouth curved and full, with a lower lip which, when he was young, could look very sulky. His hair was thick and straight, and he wore it long, tapered down the back of his neck on to his collar, and used as I was to the hair fashions of Reef Point, either crew cut (surfers) or shoulder length (hippies), I thought the effect was very attractive. He wore that morning a blue shirt with a cotton handkerchief knotted in the open neck and a pair of washed-out cord trousers hitched round his waist with a belt of plaited wool.

I said, fishing for confirmation of what I hoped was true, "Are you really on leave?"

"Of course," he said shortly, confirming nothing.

I resigned myself to never knowing. "You're with an advertising firm?"

"Yes. Strutt and Seward. P.A. to the Managing Director."

"Is that a good job?"

"It includes an expense account."

"You mean boozey lunches with prospective clients."

"It doesn't have to be a boozey lunch. If the prospective client is pretty, it's just as likely to be an intimate candle-lit supper."

A twinge of jealousy had to be firmly battened down. I was at the dressing-table now, combing out the long heavy tassel of my hair, and he said, without any change of expression, "I'd forgotten how long it was. You used to wear it in plaits. It's like silk."

"Every now and then I swear I'm going to get it cut off, but I never get round to it." I finished my hair and laid down the comb and went to join him on the bed, kneeling to open the window and hang out.

"Delicious smell," I told him. "All damp and autumny."

"Doesn't California smell damp and autumny?"

"Most of the time it smells of petrol." I thought of Reef Point. "When it isn't smelling of gum trees and the Pacific."

"And how is life with the Redskins?"

I shot him a sharp look, daring him to start being offensive, and he relented. "Honestly Jane, I was terrified you'd come back chewing gum and slung with cameras, and say 'Gee, Sin' every time you addressed a remark in my direction."

"You're out of date, brother," I told him.

"Protesting, then, you know, with a picket saying, 'Make Love Not War'." He said this in a fake American accent which I found as tedious as being kidded in California about my terribly terribly British voice.

I told him so and added, "I promise you that when I start protesting, you will be the first to know."

He acknowledged this with a wicked gleam. "How's your father?"

"He's grown a beard and he looks like Hemingway."

"I can imagine." A pair of mallards flew down out of the sky, came in to land on the water, with that little scud of white foam, just as they touched down. We watched them and then Sinclair yawned and stretched and gave me a brotherly slap and said it was time for breakfast, so we got up off the bed and closed the window again and went downstairs.

I found that I was ravenous. There was bacon, and eggs and Cooper's marmalade and hot floury rolls which I remembered were called baps, and while I ate, Sinclair and my grandmother talked, in a desultory fashion—breakfast chat concerning news in the local paper, the result of a flower show, a letter that my grandmother had received from an elderly cousin who had gone to live in a place called Mortar.

"What the hell's he gone to live there for?"

"Well, it's cheap of course, and warm. The poor old thing always suffered dreadfully from rheumatics."

"And how does he propose passing his days? Rowing sightseers around Grand Harbour?"

I realized that they were talking about Malta. Mortar: Malta. I was more Americanized than I had thought.

My grandmother poured coffee. I watched her and worked out that she must now be in her seventies, but she still looked exactly as I had always remembered her. She was tall, dignified and very good looking, her white hair always immaculate, her eyes, deep set beneath finely arched eyebrows, a bright and piercing blue. (At the moment their effect was charmingly youthful, but I knew that she could register a world of disapproval with a single lift of those eyebrows, accompanied by a chilling blue stare.) Her clothes were ageless too, and entirely becoming. Soft heathery tweed skirts and cashmere sweaters or cardigans. In the day-time she wore constantly her pearls, and a pair of coral earrings, shaped like tear drops. In the evenings a modest diamond or two was likely to spark from her dark velvets, for she was sufficiently old-fashioned to change each evening for dinner, even if it was Sunday and we ate nothing more exciting than scrambled eggs.

And as she sat ensconced at the head of her table, I thought that she had had more than her share of tragedy. Her husband had died, and then she had lost her daughter and now her son, the elusive Aylwyn, who had chosen to live and die in Canada. Sinclair and I were all she had left. And Elvie. But her back remained straight and her manner brisk, and I was thankful that she would never become one of those mournful old ladies, perpetually remembering the old days. She was too interested, too active, too intelligent. Indestructible, I told myself comfortably. That's what she is. Indestructible.

After breakfast Sinclair and I made a ritual tour of the island, missing nothing. We went out through the gate that leads into the graveyard. There we did the rounds of all the old headstones, and peered in through the window-gaps of the ruined church, and then climbed the wall into the field, and went down past the eyes of curious cattle, to the edge of the loch. We disturbed a pair of mallard ducks and had a competition skimming flat stones, seeing who could throw them the farthest. Sinclair won. We walked the length of the jetty to look at the leaky old boat that was such a devil to row, and our footsteps echoed out over the sagging planking.

"One day," I said, "this is going to collapse."

"No point in getting it mended if it's never used."

We went on, around the edge of the water, under the spreading beech where we had built our tree house, and then up through the birch spinney, ringed about by quietly falling leaves, and so back to the house by way of a cluster of out-buildings—abandoned piggeries and henhouses, and stables, and an old coach house which had long since been put to use as a garage.

"Come and see my car," said Sinclair.

We struggled with bolts and the big, old-fashioned door, and it swung creakily back to reveal, alongside my grandmother's large and dignified Daimler, a dark yellow Lotus Elan, black hooded, low to the ground and infinitely lethal.

I said, "How long have you had that?"

"Oh, about six months." He got in behind the driving wheel, and backed it out, the engine purring like an angry tiger, and showed me, like a small boy with a new toy, the car's varied accomplishments: the electrically operated windows; the neat device which worked the hood; the automatic burglar alarm; the headlight covers, which opened and shut like monstrous eyelids.

"How fast does it go?" I enquired nervously.

He shrugged. "Hundred and twenty, hundred and thirty?"

"Not with me in it, you don't."

"Wait until you're invited, my chicken-hearted child."

"You couldn't go sixty on the roads up here without coming off them altogether." He got out of the car. "Aren't you going to put it away?"

"No." He glanced at his watch. "I've got a date to shoot pigeons." I knew I was home. In Scotland men perpetually go and shoot things regardless of any plans their womenfolk may have made for them.

I said, "When'll you be back?"

"Probably for tea." He grinned down at me. "Tell you what, after tea, I'll walk you up to call on the Gibsons. They can't wait to see you and I promised I would."

"All right. Let's do that."

We went back to the house, Sinclair to change and collect all his shooting clobber, and me to go up to my room and unpack.

As I went in through the door the air struck chill and I shivered and realized that already I was missing the Californian sunshine and American central heating. Elvie was thick-walled and south-facing.

Open fires burned constantly and there were always gallons of hot water, but the bedrooms were inclined to be decidedly parky. I laid my clothes in the empty drawers and came to the conclusion that although they were Mild-Wash, Drip-Dry and Perma-Pressed, they were not warm. For Scotland I should have to buy some new ones. Perhaps— happy thought—my grandmother would buy them for me.

With this in mind I went downstairs to find her, and met her coming out of the kitchen wearing rubber boots and an ancient rain- coat and carrying a basket.

She said, "I was just coming to look for you. Where's Sinclair?"

"Gone pigeon shooting."

"Oh, yes, he said he'd be out for lunch. Come and help me pick sprouts."

Our progress was held up for a moment while I found boots and an old coat and then we set out once more into the quiet morning, only this time we made for the walled garden. Will, the gardener, was there already. He looked up as we came in, stopped digging and came tread- ing cannily over the newly-turned earth to shake me, muddily, by the hand.

"Eh," he said, "itsh a long time since you were lasht at Elvie." He did not always speak very clearly, as he only wore his teeth on Sundays. "And hoo is life in America?"

I told him a little about life in America, and he asked for my father, and I asked for Mrs Will, who appeared to be ailing, as always, and then he went back to his digging and my grandmother and I went off to pick sprouts.

When we had filled the basket, we went back towards the house, but the morning was so fresh and quiet that Grandmother said she didn't want to go back indoors just yet, so we went around and into the garden, and sat on a white-painted, iron seat, looking out over the garden and the water, to the mountains beyond. The herbaceous bor- der was filled with dahlias and zinnias and purple Michaelmas daisies, and the pearly grass was scattered with the dark red leaves of a Cana- dian maple.

She said, "I always think autumn is a perfect time. Some people think it's sad, but it's really much too beautiful to be sad."

I quoted,

"September has come, it is her's,
     Whose vitality leaps in the autumn."

"Who wrote that?"

"Louis MacNeice. Does your vitality leap?"

"Well, it might have done twenty years ago." We laughed and she pressed my hand. "Oh, Jane, what a delight to have you back again."

"You wrote so often and I would have come before . . . but it really wasn't possible."

"No, of course not, I quite see that. And it was selfish of me to keep insisting."

"And those . . . letters you wrote to my father. I didn't know anything about them, or I'd have made him reply."

"He was always a very stubborn man." She shot me a glance, very sharp and blue. "He didn't want you to come?"

"I'd made up my mind. He became resigned. Besides, with David Stewart there, waiting to bring me, he could scarcely raise too many objections."

"I was afraid you wouldn't be able to leave him."

"No." I reached down and picked up a maple leaf and started shredding it between my fingers. "No. He has a friend staying with him."

Again that sideways glance. "A friend?"

I looked up ruefully. She had always been high-principled, but never a prude. I said, "Linda Lansing. She's an actress. And his current girl-friend."

After a little, "I see," said my grandmother.

"No, I don't think you probably do. But I like her, and she'll look after him . . . anyway, until I get home again."

"I can't think," said my grandmother, "why he didn't marry again."

"Perhaps because he didn't stay in any one place long enough for the banns to be called?"

"But it's selfish. It hasn't given you a chance to get away, come back and see us all, or even to have some sort of a career."

"A career is one thing I have never wanted."

"But nowadays every girl should be able to support herself."

I said that I was very happy being supported by my father, and my grandmother said I was as stubborn as he was and hadn't I ever wanted to do some sort of a job?

I thought hard, but could only remember being eight years old and wanting to join a circus and help wash the camels. I did not think my grandmother would appreciate this, so I said, "Not really."

"Oh, my poor Jane."

I rose like a bird to my father's defence. "Not poor. Not poor anything. I don't feel I've missed a thing." But I added, to soften this, "Except Elvie. I did miss Elvie. And you. And everything." She made no comment on this. I dropped the shredded leaf, and stooped to pick up another. I said, intent on it, "David Stewart told me about Uncle Aylwyn. I didn't say anything to Sinclair . . . but . . . I was sorry . . . I mean, his being so far away and everything."

"Yes." Her voice was expressionless. "But then, that's what he chose . . . to live in Canada, and finally, to die there. You see, Elvie never meant very much to Aylwyn. He was essentially a restless person. He needed, more than anything, the company of a lot of different people. He liked variety in everything he did. And Elvie was never the best place for that."

"It's strange . . . a man being bored in Scotland . . . it's so essentially a man's ambience."

"Yes, but you see, he didn't like shooting, and he never wanted to fish, he was bored by it. He liked horses and racing. He was a great racing man."

I realized, with some surprise, that this was the first time we had spoken about my Uncle Aylwyn. It was not exactly that the subject had been avoided; just that, before, I had been totally incurious. But now I realized it was unnatural how little I knew about him . . . I did not even know how he had looked, for my grandmother, unlike most women of her generation, was not one for family photographs. Any that she had were neatly filed away in albums, not standing about, silver-framed, on top of the grand piano.

I said, "What sort of a person was he? What did he look like?"

"Look like? He looked like Sinclair does now. And he was very charming . . . he would walk into a room and you could see all the women perk up, and start smiling and being very attractive. It was quite amusing to watch."

I was on the point of asking about Silvia, but she forestalled me by glancing at her watch, and turning businesslike again.

"Now, I must go and give these sprouts to Mrs Lumley or she won't get them in time for lunch. Thank you for helping me pick them. And I've enjoyed our little talk."

Sinclair, true to his word, was home for tea. Afterwards, we put on coats and whistled up the dogs and set off to call on the Gibsons.

They lived in a small keeper's cottage, tucked into a fold of the hill which rose to the north of Elvie, so that we had to walk off the island, and cross the main road, and follow a track which wound up between grass and heather, crossing and re-crossing a tumbling burn which passed under the road by means of a culvert and emptied itself into Elvie Loch. It had traveled from deep and high in the mountains, and the glen down which it ran, and the hills on either side, were all part of my grandmother's estate.

In the old days, there had been shooting parties, with schoolchildren as beaters, and hill ponies to carry elderly gentlemen up to their butts, but now the moor was let off to a syndicate of local business men, who enjoyed walking the moor during two or three Saturdays in August but appeared just as well content to bring their families picnicking, or to fish the waters of the burn.

As we approached the cottage, there was a cacophony of barking from the kennels, and, disturbed by the noise, the figure of Mrs Gibson presently appeared through the open door. Sinclair waved and called, "Hello there!" and Mrs Gibson waved back, and then disappeared hastily back inside again.

"Gone to put the kettle on?" I suggested.

"Or warn Gibson to put his teeth in."

"That's not at all kind."

"No. But likely."

There was an old Land-Rover parked by the side of the house with half a dozen white Leghorn hens pecking round its wheels and a line of breeze-stiffened washing. As we came up to the door, Mrs Gibson came out once more, having removed her apron. She wore a blouse with a cameo brooch at the collar and was beaming from ear to ear.

"Oh, Miss Jane, I'd have known you anywhere. I was speaking to Will, and he said you hadna' changed at a'. And Mr Sinclair . . . I didn't know you were up."

"Taken a few days' leave."

"Come away in then, Gibson's just taking his tea."

"I hope we've not come at a bad time. . . ." Sinclair stood aside and waited for me to go ahead of him. I ducked my head cannily at the door, and went into the kitchen, where a fire burned redly in the grate and Gibson was heaving himself to his feet from behind a table laden with scones, cakes, butter and jam, tea and milk, and a comb of honey. There was also a strong smell of haddock.

"Oh, Gibson, we *are* disturbing you . . ."

"Not at all, not at all . . ." He put out his hand and I took it, and it felt dry and gnarled as old tree bark. Without his inevitable tweed hat he looked strange and unfamiliar, as vulnerable as a policeman without his helmet, his bald head protected by only a few wisps of white hair. And I realized that, of all my friends at Elvie, he was the only one who had truly aged. His eyes were pale and rimmed with white. He was thinner, more stooped, his voice had lost its manly depth.

"Aye, we haird you were on your way home." He turned as Sinclair followed us into the hot, crowded little room. "An' you, too, Sinclair."

"Hello, Gibson."

Mrs Gibson bustled in behind him, organizing us all. "He's just having his tea, Sinclair, but you can just sit down for a wee while, Gibson willna mind. Now, you sit here, Jane, near the fire where it's nice and warm . . ." I sat, so close to the heat I thought I would roast. ". . . would you like a cup of tea?"

"Yes, I'd love one."

"And a wee bit to eat." She made for the scullery, laying a hand on her husband's shoulder as she passed behind him, and pressing him back on to his chair. "Sit down, dearie, and finish your haddock, Jane won't mind . . ."

"Yes, please finish it."

But Gibson said that he had had enough, and Mrs Gibson whisked away his plate as though it were indecent, and went off to fill her kettle. Sinclair pulled a chair out from the other side of the table, and sat down, facing Gibson across the electro-plated cake stand. He took out his cigarettes and gave the old keeper one and took one for himself, and then leaned across to light it.

"How've you been?" he asked.

"Oh, no' so bad . . . it's been a braw, dry summer. I hear you were after the pigeons today—how did you get on?"

They talked, and listening to their conversation and seeing them thus, the young strong man, and the old one, it was hard to remember that once Gibson had been the only man the boy Sinclair really respected.

Mrs Gibson bustled back with two clean cups—her best, I realized —and set them on the table, and poured tea, and offered us scones, iced "fancies" and shortbread, all of which we tactfully refused. Then she settled herself down on the opposite side of the fireplace and we gossiped cosily, and once more I was asked for news of my father, and gave it, and then I asked after her sons, and was told that Hamish was in the army, but George had managed to get into Aberdeen University where he was reading Law.

I was very impressed. "But that's wonderful. I never knew he was as clever as that!"

"He was always a very hard-working boy . . . a great one for the books."

"So neither Hamish nor George will follow their father."

"Och, it's not the same for the young ones. They don't want to spend their lives on the hill in all weathers . . . it's too quiet for them. And mind, you can't blame them. It's no life for a young man these days, and while we managed to bring them up all right, there's not the money in it these days. Not when they can earn three times as much with a job in a city, or a factory, or an office."

"Does Gibson mind?"

"No." She looked at him fondly, but he was too involved with Sinclair to notice her glance. "No, he was always anxious that they should do what they wanted, and do well for themselves. He encouraged Geordie all the way . . . and mind," added Mrs Gibson, unconsciously quoting Barrie, "there's nothing like a good education."

"Haven't you got pictures of them? I'd love to see how they look."

She was delighted at being asked. "I have them by my bed. I'll go and fetch them . . ."

She bustled off, and I heard her footsteps, heavytreaded, up the little staircase, and across the floor of the room above. Behind me, Gibson was saying, "Mind, there's nothing wrong with the old butts . . . when they were built, they were built to last . . . they're just a wee bit overgrown."

"And the birds?"

"Aye, there are ony number of birds. Mind, I got a couple of vixen and their cubs during the spring."

"What about cows?"

"I've kept them awa'. And the heather's great, it was well burnt at the beginning of the season. . . ."

"You're not finding it too much for you?"

"Och, I'm fit enough yet."

"My grandmother said you had a week or two in bed last winter."

"That was just a touch of the flu. The doctor gave me a bottle and

I was richt as rain . . . you don't need to listen to what the women say. . . ."

Mrs Gibson, returning with the photographs, picked this up.

"What's that about women?"

"You're just a lot of auld hens," her husband told her. "Fussing over a wee bit flu . . ."

"Ach, it wisna so wee . . . and whit a time I had to keep him in bed," she added for Sinclair's benefit. She handed the photographs over for me to study, and warmed to the subject. "And I'm not so sure it was just flu . . . I wanted him to have an X-ray, but he wouldn't hear of it."

"You should, Gibson."

"Ach, I havna' time to be going to Inverness for all that caper . . ." and, as if bored by the subject of his health and wishing to change the subject, he shifted his chair in my direction in order to peer over my shoulder at the photographs of his sons; Hamish, a solid looking corporal in the Camerons, and George, formally posed in a photographer's salon. "Geordie's at the University, did Mrs Gibson tell you? In his third year now, and he'll end up a lawyer. Do you mind the time he helped you build yon tree house?"

"It's still standing, too. It hasn't blown down yet."

"Onything Geordie did, he always did well. He's a great lad."

We stayed to gossip a little longer, and then Sinclair pushed back his chair and said that it was time to go. The Gibsons came out to see us off, and the dogs, hearing voices again, started up their barking, so we all went over to the kennels to talk to them. There were two, both bitches, one black and the other gold. The one had a soft, creamy coat, and an endearing expression, with dark tip-tilted eyes.

I said, "She looks like Sophia Loren."

"Oh, aye," said Gibson. "She's bonnie. She's on season just now, so I'm taking her over to Braemar tomorrow. There's a man there with a good dog. I thought maybe we'd see if we could get a litter of pups."

Sinclair raised his eyebrows. "You're going tomorrow? What time?"

"I'll be leaving around the back end of nine."

"What's the weather forecast? What sort of a day is it going to be?"

"We should have a bit of a wind tonight, blow all this murk away. It's a good forecast for the weekend."

Sinclair turned to smile at me. "What do you say?"

I had been playing with the dog and scarcely listening to all this. "Uh?"

"Gibson's going to Braemar tomorrow morning. We could get a lift, walk back home through the Lairig Ghru . . ." He turned back to Gibson. "Could you get up to Rothiemurchus in the evening and meet us?"

"Oh aye, I could do that. About what time would that be?"

Sinclair considered. "About six? We should be in by then." He looked at me again. "What do you say, Jane?"

I had never walked the Lairig Ghru. In the old days, every summer, it had been done by someone from Elvie, and I always longed to go, but was never included in the party because my legs were not considered sufficiently long. But now . . .

I looked up at the sky. The cloud of the morning had never cleared and was now turning, as the day died, to a fine mist. "Is it really going to be a good day?"

"Oh, aye, and verra warm."

Gibson's opinion was enough. "I'd like to do it. More than anything."

"Well that's settled. Nine o'clock at the house then?"

"I'll be there," promised Gibson, and we thanked them for the tea and left them, walking down the hill and across the wet road, and so to Elvie. The dank air hung with moisture and beneath the copper beeches it was very dark. I was suddenly depressed. I had wanted nothing to change . . . had wanted Elvie to be exactly as I remembered it, but seeing Gibson, so aged, had brought me up with a jolt. He had been ill, he said. One day he would die. And the thought of death, in that chill, in-between hour, made me shiver.

Sinclair said, "Cold?"

"I'm all right. It's been a long day."

"Are you sure you want to go tomorrow? It's a hell of a walk."

"Yes, of course." I yawned. "We'll have to get Mrs Lumley to give us a picnic."

We came out from under the beeches and the forbidding north aspect of the house reared before us, silhouetted against the lowering sky. A single light burned, shining yellow across the blue dusk. And I decided that before dinner I would have a hot bath, and then I would not feel cold and depressed any longer.

Chapter 6

I WAS RIGHT. Lapped in silky Scottish water, I dozed. It was still early, so I found a hot water bottle in the bathroom cupboard and filled it from the tap and went to bed for an hour, lying in the darkness with the curtains undrawn and listening to the endless honking and gabbling of the wild geese.

After this, I dressed again, and with a vague idea of making my first night home something of an occasion, took trouble to pile up my hair and to use every sort of artifice on my eyes. Then I took down my only formal garment, a gold-and-black caftan in heavy silk, all embroidered and frogged in gold, which my father had found in an obscure Chinese shop in a back street of San Francisco and had been unable to resist.

It made me look very regal. I fixed on my earrings, splashed some scent around and went downstairs. I was early, but I wanted to be early. As I lay in bed, I had made a small plan and wanted the place to myself.

My grandmother's drawing-room, made ready for the evening, had an impact as visually charming as a stage set. The velvet curtains had been closed against the darkness, the cushions plumped, magazines straightened, and the fire made up. The room was softly lit by a pair of lamps, and flamelight was reflected in brass fender and coal shuttle, and from lovingly polished wooden surfaces all over the room. There were flowers everywhere, and boxes filled with cigarettes, and the small table which did duty as a bar was neatly lined up with bottles and glasses, an ice bucket and a small dish of nuts.

Over on the other side of the room, flanking the fireplace, was a highly decorated bombé cabinet, with glassfronted bookshelves on top, and three deep, heavy drawers beneath. I went over to this, and pushing a small table out of the way, knelt to open the bottom drawer. One of the handles had broken and the drawer was very heavy, and I was struggling with it when I heard the door open again and someone came in. Feeling foiled, I swore to myself, but there wasn't time to get to my feet before a voice said, from just behind me, "Good evening."

It was David Stewart. I looked up over my shoulder, and found him standing over me, looking unexpectedly romantic in a dark blue dinner jacket.

I was too surprised to be polite. "I'd completely forgotten you were coming for dinner."

"I'm afraid I'm a little early. There didn't seem to be anyone around, so I let myself in. What are you doing? Looking for an earring, or playing bears?"

"Neither. I'm trying to get this drawer open."

"What for?"

"It used to be full of photograph albums. Judging from the weight, I should guess it still is."

"Let me have a go."

I moved obediently aside, and watched while he doubled up on his long legs, took hold of the two handles, and gently eased the drawer open.

"It looks so easy," I said, "when someone else does it."

"Are these what you are looking for?"

"That's right." There were three of them, old, bulging albums, weighing a ton.

"Did you intend indulging in a long, nostalgic session? With this lot it should take you the rest of the evening."

"No, of course not. But I want to find a picture of Sinclair's father . . . I thought perhaps there'd be a wedding group."

There was a small silence. Then, "Why this sudden desire to find a photograph of Aylwyn Bailey?"

"Well, it seems ridiculous, but I've never seen one. I mean, Grandmother never had any standing around. I don't think there's even one in her room . . . I don't remember it. It's funny, isn't it?"

"Not necessarily. Not when you know her."

I decided to take him into my confidence. "We were talking about him today. She said that he looked like Sinclair, and that he was very charming. She said that he only had to walk into a room for all the women to start falling about in heaps. I never paid him much heed when I was little . . . he was simply Sinclair's father-in-Canada. But . . . I don't know . . . I suddenly got all curious."

I lifted out the first book, and opened it, but it was dated only ten years ago, so I went down to the bottom of the drawer, and took out the last one. It was a handsome album, bound in leather, and all the photographs—faded now and inclined to be sepia coloured—had been entered with geometrical precision and labelled in white ink.

I leafed through the pages. Shooting parties and picnics, and groups, and studio portraits, complete with painted backdrops and potted palms. A girl in presentation feathers, and a black-stockinged child (my mother) dressed as a gipsy.

And then a wedding group. "This is it." My grandmother, stately in what looked like a velvet turban and a very long dress. My mother, smiling gaily as though determined to look as though she were enjoying herself. My father, young and slim, clean shaven and wearing his suffering expression. Probably his collar was too tight. An unknown child being a bridesmaid, and finally, the bride and groom. Silvia and Aylwyn, their young faces round and curiously untouched by any sort of experience. Silvia with a little, painted, dark-red mouth and Aylwyn smiling in a private way at the camera, his tip-tilted eyes suggesting that the whole business was the most enchanting joke.

"Well?" said David at last.

"Grandmother was right . . . he's exactly like Sinclair . . . it's just that his hair's shorter and cut differently, and perhaps he's not quite so tall. And Silvia—" I didn't like Silvia— "Silvia left him after they'd only been married about a year. Did you know that?"

"Yes, I knew."

"That's why Sinclair was always at Elvie. What are you doing?"

He was feeling around in the back of the drawer. "Here are some more," he said, and brought out a pile of heavily mounted photographs which had been put away at the back and out of sight.

"What are they?" I laid down the book I had been holding.

He turned them over in his hand. "Yet another wedding. At a guess, I'd say your grandmother's."

Aylwyn was forgotten. "Oh, let me see."

We were back now into the years of the First World War, hobble skirts and enormous hats. The group was posed around on chairs, like Royalty; high collars and cut-away coats, and expressions on faces of enormous solemnity. My grandmother as a young bride was large-bosomed, and draped in lace, her new husband scarcely older than she

57

was, with that same amused, merry expression which even his sombre clothes and considerable moustache could do nothing to quench.

I said, "Here, he looks gay."

"I think he probably was."

"And who's this? The old fellow in whiskers and a kilt?"

David looked over my shoulder. "Probably the bridegroom's father. Isn't he splendid?"

"Who was he?"

"I believe a great character—called himself Bailey of Cairneyhall —they were an old family around here, and legend has it that he used to give himself tremendous airs and graces, despite the fact that he didn't have a ha'penny to bless himself with."

"And my grandmother's father?"

"That impressive looking gentleman, I imagine. Now, he was a very different kettle of fish. A stockbroker in Edinburgh. He made a lot of money and died a rich man. And your grandmother," he added in lawyer-like tones, "was his only child."

"You mean . . . she was an heiress."

"You could say that."

I looked at the picture again, the solemn, unfamiliar faces who were my ancestors, the people who had made me, with all my faults and my small talents, and had given me my face and my freckles, and my fair Nordic hair.

"I never even heard of Cairneyhall."

"You wouldn't. It became so derelict and ramshackle it eventually had to be pulled down."

"So my grandmother never lived there?"

"I think for a year or two she did, probably in the greatest possible discomfort. But when her husband died, she moved to this part of the world, bought Elvie, and brought her children up here."

"So . . ." I stopped. I realized that, without ever having thought very much about it, I had always taken it for granted that my grandmother was if not exactly "richly left," then certainly well provided for. But it seemed now that this was not so. Elvie, and everything in it, had come from her own inheritance, belonged solely to her. And it had no connection whatsoever with her marriage to Aylwyn's father.

David was watching me. "So?" he prompted gently.

"Nothing." I was embarrassed. The whole question of money makes me feel uncomfortable, a trait I have inherited from my father, and I hastily changed the subject. "How do you know so much about them all, anyway?"

"Because I look after the family affairs."

"I see."

He closed the photograph album. "Perhaps we'd better put them all away . . ."

"Yes, of course. And, David . . . I don't want Grandmother to know I've been asking all these questions."

"I won't say a word."

We put the books and the photographs back where we had found them, and closed the drawer. I moved the table back into its place, then went to take the guard from in front of the fire, and find a cigarette, and light it with a spill. As I straightened, I found David watching me. He said, out of the blue, "You're looking very beautiful. Scotland obviously agrees with you."

I said, "Thank you," which is what nicely raised American girls are taught to say when paid a compliment. (English girls say things like, "Oh, I don't, I look a mess", or "How can you say you like this dress? It's ghastly", which I am assured can be very off-putting.)

And then, because I felt suddenly shy and needed a diversion, I suggested that I should fix him a drink, and he said that in Scotland one didn't fix drinks, one poured them.

"Not martinis," I insisted. "You can't pour a martini until you've fixed it. It stands to reason."

"You have a point. Do you want a martini?"

I was doubtful. "Do you know how to make one?"

"I like to think so."

"My father says only two men in Britain can make a martini, and he's one of them."

"Then I must be the other." He went over to the table and busied himself amongst the bottles and ice and twists of lemon peel. He said, "What have you been doing today?"

I told him, right up to the hot bath and the session on my bed, and then I said, "And tomorrow you couldn't guess what we've planned."

"No, I couldn't. Tell me."

"Sinclair and I are going to walk the Lairig Ghru."

He was gratifyingly impressed. "Are you *really?*"

"Yes, really. Gibson's going to drive us over to Braemar and then meet us at Rothiemurchus in the evening."

"What sort of day is it going to be?"

"Gibson says fine. He says all this murk's going to blow away and it'll be 'verra hot'." I watched him, liking his brown hands, and his dark neat head, and the wide shoulders beneath the soft blue velvet. I said, on an impulse, "You should come too . . ."

He came across the room, carrying the two pale golden, icy drinks. "I'd like to more than anything, but I'm busy all day tomorrow."

I took the glass and said, "Perhaps another time."

"Yes, perhaps."

We smiled, raised glasses, drank. The martini was delicious, cold and heady as fire. I said, "I'll write and tell my father I've met the other martini-mixer," and then I remembered something. "David, I simply have to get some clothes . . ."

He took the abrupt change of subject in his stride. "What sort of clothes?"

"Scottish clothes, sweaters and things. I've got that money my father gave me, but it's all in dollar bills. Do you think you could get them changed for me?"

"Yes, of course, but where do you intend doing your shopping? Caple Bridge isn't exactly the fashion centre of the north."

"I don't want anything fashionable, I just want something warm."

"In that case I suppose it would be all right. When do you want to do this shopping?"

"Saturday?"

"Can you drive your grandmother's car?"

"I can drive it, but I'm not allowed to. I haven't got a British licence . . . but it doesn't matter, I'll catch the bus . . ."

"All right. Then come to the office—I'll tell you how to find it— and I'll give you your money, and then when you've fixed yourself up with woollies, and if you haven't anything better to do, I'll give you lunch."

"Will you?" I had not expected this, and I was delighted. "Where?"

He scratched thoughtfully at the back of his neck. "There's not really much choice. Either the Crimond Arms, or my house, and my housekeeper doesn't come in on a Saturday."

I said, "I can cook. You buy something and I'll cook it. Anyway, I'd like to see where you live."

"It's not very exciting."

But I found that I was mildly excited, all the same. I have always thought that you don't know a man until you have seen his home, his books, his pictures, the way he fixes his furniture. David, all that time in California, and while we were travelling home together, had been sweet and kind, but had shown me only the correct and businesslike side of his character. But now he had helped me find the photograph I wanted, and answered, with great patience, all my questions, and finally asked me out to lunch. I realized that there was a great deal more to him than I had first thought, and it was enormously gratifying to imagine that perhaps he felt the same way about me.

By the end of dinner I was overcome once more by fatigue, or jet-lag or whatever you like to call it, and using my energetic day tomorrow as an excuse, I said good night to the others, and went to bed where I immediately fell sound asleep.

I awoke, some time later, to the sound of the wind that Gibson had promised us, nudging at the house, whistling under my door, whipping up the waters of the loch into small waves which broke and splashed against the shingle. And, above the sounds of the night, I heard voices.

I reached for my watch, saw that it was not yet midnight, and listened again. The voices became clearer and I realized then that they belonged to my grandmother and Sinclair, and that they were out on the lawn below my room, doubtless taking the dogs for a turn around the garden before locking the house up for the night.

". . . thought he'd aged a lot." That was Sinclair.

"Yes, but what can one do?"

"Pension him off. Get another man."

"But where would they go? It's not as though either of the boys were married, with a home to give them. Besides, he's been here for nearly fifty years . . . as long as I have. I couldn't get rid of him just because he's getting old. Anyway, he'd be dead in two months without a job of work to do."

I realized, uncomfortably, that they were talking about Gibson.

"But he's not able to do this particular job any longer."

"Now, what grounds have you got for saying that?"

"It's obvious. He's past it."

"As far as I'm concerned, he's still perfectly adequate. It's not as though he were expected to run a lot of highly-powered shoots. The syndicate is—"

Sinclair interrupted her. "That's another thing. It's utterly im-

practical letting off a superb moor like this to one or two local businessmen from Caple Bridge. What they pay you doesn't even begin to
cover Gibson's keep."

"The one or two local businessmen, Sinclair, happen to be my
friends."

"That's beside the point. As far as I can see, we seem to be running some sort of charitable institution."

There was a pause, and then, coldly, my grandmother corrected
him. "*I* seem to be running some sort of charitable institution."

The iciness of her voice would have silenced me, but Sinclair
seemed impervious to it, and I wondered how much of his courage was
the Dutch variety, bolstered by post-prandial brandies.

"In that case," he said, "I suggest that you stop. Now. Pension
Gibson off and sell the moor, or at least let it to a syndicate that is able
to afford to pay a reasonable rent . . ."

"I have told you already . . ."

Their voices faded. They were walking away, still deeply in discussion; they went round the corner of the house, and I could hear
them no longer. I found that I was lying rigid in my bed, miserable at
having been forced to hear what was obviously not intended for my
ears. The thought of them quarrelling made me sick, but worse was
what they quarrelled about.

Gibson. I thought of him as he used to be, strong and tireless, and
a mine of countryman's lore and wisdom. I remembered him, endlessly
patient, teaching Sinclair to shoot and fish, answering questions, letting us tag along at his heels like a pair of puppies. And Mrs Gibson,
who had spoiled and petted us, bought us sweets and fed us scones hot
from her oven, dripping with the strong yellow butter that she churned
herself.

It was impossible to reconcile the past with the present—the Gibson I remembered and the old man I had seen today. And harder still
to realize that it was my cousin Sinclair who spoke so glibly of getting
rid of Gibson, as if he were a smelly old dog, and the time had come at
last to have him painlessly put down.

Chapter 7

I AWOKE AGAIN, drawn from sleep by some subconscious alarm. I knew it was daylight. I stirred and opened my eyes, and a man was standing at the foot of my bed, watching me, cold-eyed. I let out a gasp of fright, and sat up with my heart pounding, but it was only Sinclair, come to wake me.

"It's eight o'clock," he said. "We have to leave at nine."

I sat rubbing the sleep out of my eyes, giving myself time to let the panic run out of my veins. "You gave me the most dreadful fright."

"Sorry, I didn't mean to . . . I was just going to wake you up . . ."

I looked up again, and this time saw no menace, simply the familiar figure of my cousin, arms crossed on the end of my bed, tip-tilted eyes dancing with amusement. He wore a faded kilt and a big ribbed pullover, with a scarf knotted at the neck. He looked clean and brushed, and smelt deliciously of the after-shave he had slapped on his face.

I scrambled into a kneeling position and hung out of the open window to inspect the day. It was perfect, bright, clean, cold, the sky cloudless. I said, in wonder, "Gibson was right."

"Of course he was right. He always is. Did you hear the wind in the night? And there's been a frost, soon all the trees will be turning."

The loch, blue with reflected sky, was flecked with small scuds of white foam, and the mountains opposite were no longer veiled in mist, but clear and sparkling, bruised with great sweeps of purple heather, and in the morning's crystal air, I could trace every rock and crack and corrie that led to their swelling summits.

It was impossible not to be elated by such a day. The uncertainties of the night had gone with the darkness. I had heard what was not intended for my ears. But in the clear light of morning, it seemed perfectly possible that I had been mistaken, had misunderstood. After all, I had not heard the beginning of the discussion, nor the end . . . and it was wrong to make any sort of a judgement when I was in possession of only half the facts.

Relief at having so easily shed my private worries made me suddenly enormously happy. I jumped off the bed, and went, in my nightdress, to find some clothes, and Sinclair, his mission successfully accomplished, went downstairs to start his breakfast.

We ate it in the kitchen, warm and snug by the Aga. Mrs Lumley had fried sausages and I ate four, and drank two enormous cups of coffee, and then I went and found an old rucksack, and we packed it with lunch: sandwiches and chocolate, apples and cheese.

"Do you want a Thermos?" Mrs Lumley wanted to know.

"No," said Sinclair, still filling himself with toast and marmalade. "Put in a couple of plastic mugs, though, and then we can drink out of the river."

There was the hooting of a car horn from outside, and presently Gibson emerged through the back door. He wore his sagging greenish tweeds, the knickerbockers enormous around his skinny calves. On his head was the old tweed hat.

"Are you ready?" he asked, obviously not expecting that we would be.

But we were. We gathered up waterproof anoraks and the rucksack of rations, bade goodbye to Mrs Lumley, and went out into that glorious morning. The air was icy inside my nose, cut deep into my lungs, made me feel as though I could jump over the house.

"But aren't we lucky?" I crowed. "It's the most perfect day."

And Gibson said, "It's all right," which, being a Scotsman, was the most enthusiastic comment he could muster.

We piled into the Land-Rover. There was room for the three of us in the front, but Gibson's dog looked nervous and in need of company, so I chose to sit in the back with her. To begin with, she wheeked and was restless and worried, but after a little became used to the lurching of the car and settled down to sleep, with her soft, velvety head across my shoe.

Gibson took the road to Braemar by way of Tomintoul, driving south over the mountains and running down into the gold and sunlit

valley of the Dee at about eleven o'clock. The river was in spate, deep
and clear as brown glass, winding through fields and farmland and
great stands of tall Scotch pine. We came to Braemar, and drove
through it, and out the other side, and on for another three miles or so
until we came to the bridge that crosses the river and leads the way to
Mar Lodge.

There we stopped and all got out, the dog was given a little run,
and Gibson went to fetch the key of the forestry gates. Then we all
went into the bar, and Sinclair and Gibson had beer, and I was given a
glass of cider.

"How much farther?" I wanted to know.

"Another four miles or so," Gibson told me. "But the road is
verra rough, maybe you'd be better in the front with us."

So I abandoned the dog, and went and sat in the front between the
two men, and the road was scarcely a road at all, simply a bulldozed
track, deeply rutted, and used by the Forestry Commission. Every now
and then we would pass a team of foresters, working with huge chain-
saws and tractors. We waved, and they waved back, and sometimes had
to back their great lorries off the track so that we could pass. The air
was filled with the piney smell of trees, and when at last we came to the
little lodge, which is used for climbers and weekend expeditions, and
got out of the Land-Rover, stiff and aching from the ride, there was
the most immense quiet. The forests, the moor and the mountains
were all about us, and only a distant trickle of water, and the soughing
of the pines far above us, broke the silence.

"I'll meet you at Loch Morlich," said Gibson. "Do you think you
can make it by six o'clock?"

"If we don't, wait for us. And if we're not in by dark, get a call
through to the Mountain Rescue." Sinclair grinned. "We'll stay on the
path, so it should be perfectly easy to find us."

"Don't go turning your ankle over," Gibson warned me. "And
have a good day."

We said that we would. We watched him get back into the car,
and turn and drive off the way we had come. The sound of his engine
died away into the immensity of the morning. I looked up at the sky,
and thought, not for the first time, that Scotland seems to have more
than its fair ration of sky . . . it sweeps and soars and appears to reach
to infinity. A pair of curlews flew over and in the distance I could hear
the baa-ing of sheep. Sinclair smiled down at me. He said, "Shall we
go?"

We walked, and Sinclair led the way, and I followed him up a path that ran alongside a burn set deep in rushes. We came to a solitary sheep farm, set about with wooden pens, and a dog came out to bark at us, and we passed the farm, and went on, and the dog retired to its kennel, and silence fell again. There were, every now and then, small patches of colour, harebells blowing, and huge purple thistles, and the dark stain of heather, humming with bees. The sun climbed up into the sky, and we peeled off our sweaters and tied them around our waists, and the path leaned upwards against the hill, and we climbed through trees and Sinclair, ahead of me, started to whistle under his breath. I remembered the tune: "Mairi's Wedding"; we had sung it as children, after tea in the drawing-room, with Grandmother playing the accompaniment on the piano.

> "Step we gaily, on we go,
> Heel for heel and toe for toe,
> Arm in arm and row on row
> All for Mairi's wedding."

We came to a bridge and a waterfall, and the waterfall was not brown, but green, the colour of Chinese jade, plunging twenty feet or more into a cauldron of pale rock. We stood on the bridge and watched it, an arc of water bright as a jewel, translucent and shot with sunlight, curving down to the boiling pool, and ringed by a miniature rainbow. I had never seen anything so lovely. Over the roar of the water I said, "Why is it that colour? Why isn't it brown?" and Sinclair told me that it was because the water here dropped fresh from the limestone peaks, and so had not become stained with peat. And we stayed for a little, until, he said that we had no time to waste, and must be on our way.

For encouragement, we sang again, each vying with the other at remembering words. We sang "The Road to the Isles", and "Westering Home", and "Come Along", which is the best marching song of all, and then our path began to climb, leading up and over the shoulder of a great mountain, and we stopped singing because we needed all our breath. The ground was thick with old heather roots and very boggy, and with every step dark mud oozed on either side of my shoes. My legs started to ache, and my back; I found that I was short of breath, and, although I would set myself the goal of this summit, and then the next, it seemed there was always another, waiting beyond. It was very disheartening.

And then, just as I was giving up hope of ever getting anywhere, there appeared, ahead of us, a black tooth of a mountain, jagged tip piercing the blue of the sky, and sheer face dropping a thousand feet or more to the foot of a narrow brown valley.

I stopped and pointed. "Sinclair, what's that?"

"The Devil's Peak." He had a map. We sat, and he opened it and flattened it against the wind and identified the surrounding peaks. Ben Vrottan and Cairn Toul, Ben Macdui, and the long ridge that led to Cairngorm.

"And this valley?"

"Glen Dee."

"And the little burn?"

"The little burn, as you call it, is the mighty Dee itself, in its early stages of course." And indeed it was ludicrous to identify this modest stream with the majestic river we had seen earlier on in the morning.

We ate some chocolate and started off again, mercifully downhill, and now we had joined the long path that leads to the Lairig Ghru itself. It wound ahead of us, a scribble of white through the brown grass, climbing gently to a distant point on the horizon where the mountains and the sky seemed to meet. We walked, and the Devil's Peak towered ahead of us and over us, and then fell behind. We walked and were alone—really alone. There were no rabbits, no hares, no deer, no grouse. No eagles. Nothing broke the silence. No living creature stirred. There was only the sound of our own footsteps, and Sinclair's whistling.

> "Plenty herring, plenty meal,
> Plenty peat to fill her creel
> Plenty bonnie bairns as weel
> That's the toast for Mairi."

Presently a house came into view, a stone bothy tucked into the foot of the hill on the opposite shore of the river.

"What's that?" I asked.

"It's a refuge hut, for climbers or walkers to use in bad weather."

"What sort of time are we making?"

"Good time."

After a little, "I'm hungry," I told him.

He grinned back at me over his shoulder.

"When we reach the hut," he promised, "we'll eat."

Later we lay supine, cushioned in blowing grass, Sinclair with his head pillowed on his sweater, me with my head pillowed on his stomach. I stared up at the empty blue sky and thought that to be with a cousin was a strange thing—at times we were as close as brother and sister, but at others there was an unease between us. I told myself that it was to do with no longer being children . . . with the fact that I found Sinclair enormously attractive, and yet this could not wholly explain an instinctive restraint, as though, somewhere in the back of my mind, a bell was warning danger.

A fly, a midge, some sort of a bug landed on my face, and I brushed it away. It landed again. I said, "Darn it."

"Darn what?" came, sleepily, from Sinclair.

"A fly."

"Where?"

"My nose."

His hand came down to brush away the fly. It rested against the curve of my jaw and stayed there, his fingers cupping my chin.

He said, "If we go to sleep we'll wake to find Gibson and the entire mountain rescue team come thundering through the pass to find us."

"We won't go to sleep."

"How can you be so sure?"

I did not reply, I could not speak about my inner tensions, the tightening of my stomach at the touch of his hand . . . the fact was that I did not know if this tightening was caused by sex or—fear? It seemed an extraordinary word to use in connection with Sinclair, but now the conversation that I had heard last night came surfacing up out of my subconscious, and I worried at it again, like a dog with an old and unsavoury bone. I told myself that I should have made a point of seeing my grandmother before coming out this morning. One look at her face, and I would have known the true lie of the land. But she had not appeared before we left, and if she was sleeping then I did not want to disturb her.

I shifted uncomfortably, and Sinclair said, "What's the matter? You're as tense as a string of wire. You must have a secret worry, some sort of a guilt complex."

"What would I have to be guilty about?"

"You tell me. Leaving Poppa perhaps?"

"Father? You must be joking."

"You mean you were quite happy, shaking the dust of Reef Point, California, off your pretty heels?"

"Not at all. But Father, at the moment, is more than well provided for, and not in the least worthy of a guilt complex."

"Then it must be something else." The ball of his thumb moved lightly over my cheek. "I know, it's the love-lorn lawyer."

"The *what?*" Now, my amazement was genuine.

"The lawyer. You know, old pawky-Rankeillour himself."

"Quoting Robert Louis Stevenson will get you nowhere . . . and I still don't know what you're talking about." But of course I did.

"David Stewart, my love. Do you know, he couldn't keep his eyes off you last night? He watched you all through dinner, with a lusty glint to his eye. I must say, you were a fairly toothsome spectacle. Where did you get that eastern-looking outfit?"

"In San Francisco, and you're being ridiculous."

"Not ridiculous at all . . . honestly, it stuck out a mile. How do you fancy the idea of being an old man's darling?"

"Sinclair, he's not old."

"I suppose about thirty-five. But so dependable, my dear." His voice took on the honeyed tones of some desiccated dowager. "And such a nice boy."

"You're being bitchy."

"So I am." And, without any change of expression, he went on, "When are you going back to America?"

I was taken off-guard. "Why?"

"Just want to know."

"A month?"

"As soon as that? I'd hoped you'd stay. Abandon Father and put down your roots in your ain countree."

"I like my father too much to abandon him. And, anyway, what would I do?"

"Take a job?"

"You sound like Grandmother. And I couldn't take a job, because I'm not qualified to do anything."

"You could be a secretary."

"No, I couldn't. Every time I try to type it always comes out red."

He said, "You could get married."

"I don't know anyone."

"You know me," said Sinclair.

His thumb, stroking my cheek, was suddenly still. After a little I sat up, and turned to look down at him. His eyes were bluer than the sky, but their clear gaze gave nothing away.

"What did you say?"

"I said 'you know me.' " His hand moved, and took hold of my wrist, ringing it easily with his fingers.

"You can't be serious."

"Can't I? All right, then let's pretend I am. What would you say?"

"Well, in the first place, it would be practically incest."

"Rubbish."

"And why me?" I warmed to my subject. "You know perfectly well that you've always thought me as plain as a pikestaff, you were forever telling me so . . ."

"Not now. You're not plain now. You've turned into a gorgeous Viking . . ."

". . . and I haven't a single talent. I can't even arrange flowers."

"Why on earth should I want you to arrange flowers?"

"And anyway, I can't believe you haven't got strings of eager females, scattered all over the country, just pining away for love of you and dreaming of the day when you'll ask them to be Mrs Sinclair Bailey."

"Maybe so," said Sinclair with maddening complacency. "But I don't want them."

I considered the idea, and despite myself, found it intriguing.

"Where would we live?"

"In London of course."

"I don't want to live in London."

"You're mad. It's the only place to live. Everything happens there."

"I like the country."

"We'll go to the country at weekends—that's what I do anyway—go and stay with friends . . ."

"And do what?"

"Potter around. Sail, maybe. Go racing . . ."

I pricked my ears. "Racing?"

"Haven't you ever been to a race meeting? It's the most exciting thing on earth." He sat up, leaning back on his elbows, so that his eyes were on a level with mine. "Am I persuading you?"

I said, "There is a small consideration that you haven't mentioned yet."

"And what is that?"

"Love."

"Love?" He smiled. "But Janey, surely we love each other. We always have done."

"But that's different."

"How different?"

"I can't explain if you don't already know."

"Try."

I sat in a troubled silence. I knew that in a way he was right. I had always loved him. As a child he had been the most important person in my life. But I was not entirely sure about the man he had become. Anxious that he should not read all this in my face, I looked down and began to tug at the tough grass, pulling out tufts by the roots, and then letting them loose, to be blown away by the wind.

I said at last, "I suppose because we've both changed. You have become a different person. And I am, virtually, an American . . ."

"Oh, Janey . . ."

"No, it's true. I've been brought up there, educated there . . . the fact that I have a British passport can't alter any of that. Or the way I feel about things."

"You're talking in circles. You know that, don't you?"

"Perhaps I am. But don't forget that this whole conversation is hypothetical anyway . . . we're arguing around an assumption . . ."

He took a deep breath as if to continue the argument and then seemed to change his mind and let it all out again on a laugh. "We could sit here all day, couldn't we, and 'tire the sun with talking'."

"Shouldn't we go?"

"Yes, we've another ten miles, at least, to cover. But we've come a long way, and for your information, that remark is meant to be ambiguous."

I smiled. He put his hand around my neck and pulled my face towards his and kissed my open, smiling mouth.

I had been half-expecting this, but still not prepared for my own panicky reaction. I had to make myself be still in his arms, wait for him to finish, and when at last he drew away, I stayed for a moment where I was, and then slowly began to gather in our rucksack the paper that had wrapped the sandwiches, the red plastic drinking mugs. All at once our solitude was frightening, and I saw the two of us, tiny as ants, the only living creatures in this vast and deserted landscape, and wondered if Sinclair had brought me today with the intention of starting his extraordinary discussion, or whether the idea of marrying was just a whim, blown up out of nothing by the wind.

I said, "Sinclair, we must go. We really must go."

His eyes were thoughtful. But he only smiled and said, "Yes," and stood up, took the rucksack from me, and turned to lead the way, on up the path towards the distant pass.

We were home by dark. The last few miles I had walked blindly, simply putting one foot in front of the other, not daring to stop, for if I had, I should never have got going again. When at last we came round the final curve of the track, and, through the trees, saw the bridge and the gate, and Gibson and the Land-Rover, waiting on the road beyond, I could scarcely believe we had actually made it. Aching in every muscle, I came up the last few yards, climbed the gate, and fell into the car, but when I tried to light a cigarette, I found that my hands were shaking.

We drove home through the blue dusk. To the east a tiny new moon, pale and fine as any eyelash, hung low in the sky. Our headlights probed the road ahead, a rabbit skittered for cover, the eyes of a roaming dog glittered like twin beads, and were gone. Across me the two men talked, but I slumped, silent in an exhaustion which was not entirely physical.

That night I was awakened by the ringing of the telephone. Its shrilling cut across my dreams and pulled me out of sleep like a hooked fish. I had no idea of the time, but, turning my head, saw that the moon hung over the loch, its reflection touching the black water with small brush strokes of silver.

The ringing continued. Dazed, I stumbled out of bed, across my room, and out on to the dark landing. The telephone was downstairs, in the library, but there was an extension upstairs as well, along a passage that led to the old nurseries, and it was for this that I made.

Some time during my half-conscious progress the ringing must have stopped, but I was too sleepy to register this, so that when I reached the telephone and picked up the receiver, a voice was already speaking. A female voice, unknown to me, but pleasantly pitched, and attractive ". . . of course I'm certain. I saw the doctor this afternoon and he says there's no doubt at all. Look, I think we should talk about this . . . I'd like to see you anyway, but I can't get away . . ."

Listening dopily, I supposed that the telephone lines had become crossed. The girl on the Caple Bridge exchange had made a mistake, or gone to sleep, or something. This call was not for us. I was about to speak, when a man's voice interrupted, and all at once I was wide awake, and clearly conscious.

"Is it really so urgent, Tessa? Can't it wait?"

Sinclair. On the other line.

"Of course it's urgent . . . we haven't any time to waste . . ." and then, less calmly, as though hysteria was not very far below the surface, "Sinclair, I'm having a baby. . . ."

I put down the receiver gently, quietly. The instrument made a tiny click and the voices were extinguished. I stood in the darkness, shivering, and then turned and made my way back to the landing and hung over the banister to listen. The stairs and the hall yawned below me, black as a well, but, from beyond the closed library door, came the unmistakable murmur of Sinclair's voice.

My feet were icy. Crawling with cold I made my way back to my room, and gently closed the door and got back into bed. Presently I heard the single ring of the telephone and knew that the call was finished, and soon after that, Sinclair came quietly upstairs. He went into his room, and there were soft sounds as he moved about, opened and shut drawers, then he came out again, and went down once more. The front door opened and closed, and moments after I heard the tiger hum of the Lotus as it drove off, down the lane, and on to the main road and away.

I found that I was trembling, as I had not done since I was a child, waking from a nightmare, and convinced there were ghosts hiding in my wardrobe.

Chapter 8

NEXT MORNING, when I went downstairs, I found my grandmother already at the breakfast table. As I bent to kiss her, she said, "Sinclair's gone to London."

"How do you know?"

"He left a letter in the hall . . ." She sorted it out from the rest of her opened mail, and handed it to me. He had used the thick writing paper with *Elvie* engraved at its head, and his writing was strong and black and full of his personality.

> "Terribly sorry, have to go south for a day or two. Should be home Monday night or Tuesday morning. Take care of yourselves while I'm away, and don't get into any sort of trouble.
> Much love
> Sinclair."

That was all. I laid down the letter, and my grandmother said, "The telephone rang last night at about half past midnight. Did you hear it?"

I went to pour coffee, thankful for a reason not to meet her eyes. "Yes, I did."

"I was going to answer it, but I was fairly sure it would be for Sinclair, so I let it ring."

"Yes . . ." I brought the full cup back to the table. "Does . . . does he often do this?"

"Oh, every now and then." She sorted out some bills. It occurred to me that she seemed as anxious as I to keep herself occupied. "He leads such a full life, and then this job he has seems to make tremendous demands on his time . . . not like being in an office from nine till five."

"No, I suppose not." The coffee was hot and strong, and helped to loose the knot of tension at the back of my neck. Encouraged by this, I said, "Perhaps it's a girl-friend."

My grandmother shot me a sharp, blue glance. But she only said, "Yes, perhaps."

I leaned my elbows on the table, and tried to sound casual. "I should think he has about a hundred. He's still the best looking thing on two legs I've ever seen. Does he ever bring them home? Have you ever met any of them . . . ?"

"Oh, sometimes when I've been in London . . . you know, he brings them for dinner, or we go to the theatre or something."

"Did you ever think he'd marry one of them?"

"You can never be sure, can you?" Her voice was cool, almost disinterested. "His life in London is so different from the one he leads when he comes up here. Elvie's sort of a rest-cure as far as Sinclair's concerned . . . he simply potters. I think he's quite glad to get away from late nights and expense-account lunches."

"So there wasn't ever anyone in particular? One you specially liked?"

My grandmother laid down her letters. "Yes, there was." She took off her spectacles, and sat, looking out of the window, across the garden to where the loch sparkled blue in the sunshine of another perfect autumn day. "He met her in Switzerland, ski-ing. I think they saw a lot of each other when she got back to London."

I said, "Ski-ing? Did you send me a photograph?"

"Did I? Oh, yes, it was New Year at Zermatt. That was where they met. I think she was taking part in some championship or other, you know these international races they have . . ."

"She must be very good."

"Oh, she is. She's quite famous . . ."

"Did you ever meet her?"

"Yes, Sinclair brought her for lunch at the Connaught when I was in town during the summer. She was a charming girl."

I took a piece of toast and started to butter it. "What's she called?"

"Tessa Faraday . . . You've probably heard of her."

I had heard of her, but not in the way my grandmother meant. I looked at the toast I was buttering, and suddenly felt that if I ate it, I should be sick.

After breakfast, I went back upstairs, took up my double folder of family photographs, and drew out the one of Sinclair that my grandmother had sent to me, and that I had arranged in my montage, so that only Sinclair showed, and his companion was hidden.

But now, I was interested only in her. I saw a small, slim girl, dark-eyed, laughing, with hair caught back from her face by a ribbon, and thick gold rings in her ears. She wore a velvet trouser-suit, banded with some sort of embroidery, and she stood in the curve of Sinclair's arm, the two of them wound and tangled by yards of festive paper streamers. She looked gay and vital, very happy, and, remembering the careful voice on the telephone last night, I was suddenly frightened for her.

The fact that Sinclair had gone so promptly south—presumably to see her—should have reassured me, but somehow it did not. His departure had been too swift and businesslike, unencumbered by any personal consideration of either my grandmother or myself. Reluctantly I was reminded of his attitude towards Gibson, when he and my grandmother discussed the old keeper's possible retirement, and I realized that, subconsciously, I had been making excuses for Sinclair.

But now it was different, and I was forced to be honest with myself. The word "ruthless" sprang to mind. Where ordinary people were concerned he could be entirely ruthless, and, torn as I was by anxiety for this unknown girl, I could only hope that he could also be compassionate.

From the hall my grandmother called me. "Jane!"

I hastily pushed the picture back in the frame, set it back on the dressing-table, and went back out on to the landing.

"Yes."

"What are you doing today?"

I went down to the half-landing and sat on the stairs, and talked to her from there . . . "I'm going shopping. I have to buy some sweaters, otherwise I'll die of cold."

"Where did you plan to go?"

"Caple Bridge."

"Darling, you can't buy anything in Caple Bridge."

"I'm sure I can buy a sweater . . ."

"I have to go to Inverness for a hospital board meeting . . . why don't I take you with me in the car?"

"Because David Steward has some money for me. He changed the dollars Father gave me. And he said he'd give me lunch."

"Oh, how kind . . . but how will you get to Caple Bridge?"

"I'll jump on a bus. Mrs Lumley says there's one every hour at the end of the road."

"Well, if you're sure," but she still sounded doubtful. Standing there, with one hand on the newel post, she took off her glasses, and looked me over carefully from beneath her finely arched brows. "You look tired, Jane. Yesterday was really too much for you after all that travelling."

"No, it wasn't. I loved it."

"I should have made Sinclair wait a day or two . . ."

"But then we might have missed the lovely weather."

"Yes. Perhaps. But I noticed you didn't eat anything for breakfast."

"I never do. Honestly."

"Well, you must make sure David gives you a proper lunch . . ." She turned away and then thought of something else, and turned back. "Oh, and Jane . . . if you are shopping, why not let me stand you a new raincoat? You should have something really warm to wear."

Despite everything, I grinned. I loved it when she ran so true to form. I said wickedly, "But what's wrong with the one I've got?"

"If you must know, it makes you look like a tinker."

"In all the ten years I've been wearing it, I've never had that said to me before."

She sighed. "You get more like your father every day," she said, and without smiling at my feeble joke, went off to her desk and wrote me a cheque which would have bought me a fur-lined, floor-length, sable-hooded raincoat, if that was what I happened to be wanting.

I waited, in brilliant sunshine, at the end of the road for the bus that would take me to Caple Bridge. I could not remember a day so bright or fresh or full of colour. It had rained a little during the night, so that everything shone newly-washed, and the damp roads reflected back the blue of the sky. The hedges were full of scarlet hips, bracken was gold, and turning leaves every colour from deep crimson to butter yellow. The air, sweeping down from the north, was cold and sweet as iced wine, with a bite to it suggesting that already, much farther north, the first snow of the winter had already fallen.

The bus came around the corner, stopped for me and I got in. It was packed with country people, heading for Caple Bridge for their weekly shopping session, and the only seat I could find was next to a fat woman with a basket on her knee. She wore a blue felt hat, and was so enormous there was only room for half of me on the seat, and every time the bus turned a corner, I was in deadly danger of being thrown off altogether.

It was five miles to Caple Bridge, and I knew the road as well as I knew Elvie itself. I had walked it, ridden on my bicycle, watched the landmarks fly by from the window of my grandmother's car. I knew the names of the people who lived in the wayside cottages . . . Mrs Dargie and Mrs Thomson, and Mrs Willie McCrae. And here was the house with the bad-tempered dog, and there the field where the flock of white goats grazed.

We came to the river, ran alongside it for half a mile or so and then the road swept into a deep S-bend in order to cross the river by means of a narrow humpbacked bridge. Up to now, nothing had apparently changed in all the years I had been away, but as the bus ground cautiously over the crest of the bridge I saw, ahead of us, a roadworks and traffic lights, and realized that considerable excavations were taking place in order to eliminate a dangerous curve.

There were signs and warnings everywhere. Hedges had been bulldozed away, leaving great scars of raw earth in their wake; men were working with picks and shovels, enormous earth removers growled away like prehistoric monsters, and over it all hung the clean and delicious smell of hot tar.

The lights were against us. We waited, engines running, and then the light went from red to green, and the bus rolled on, down the narrow track between the warning signals, and back on to the road. The woman next to me began to shift about, checking the contents of her basket, looking up at the luggage rack.

I said, "Do you want something?"

"Did I put my umbrella up there?"

I stood up and delved for the umbrella, and gave it to her, also a large cardboard box of eggs, and a bundle of shaggy asters, inexpertly wrapped in newspaper. By the time all this had been collected and delivered, we had reached our destination. The bus made a huge turn around the town hall, rolled into the market square and came to a final halt.

Because I had no baskets or encumbrances, I was one of the first out. My grandmother had told me the whereabouts of the lawyers' office, and from where I stood, I could see the square stone building she had described, directly opposite me, across the cobbled market place.

Waiting for the passing traffic, I crossed over and went in through the door, and read the indicator board in the hall and saw that Mr D. Stewart could be found in room No. 3 and that he was IN. I went up a dark staircase, nicely decorated in sludge green and mud brown, passed beneath a stained-glass window that let in no light at all, and finally knocked on a door.

He said, "Come in."

I went in and was delighted to find that his office, at least, was light, bright, and had a carpet. The window looked out over the busy market square, there was a jug of Michaelmas daisies on the marble mantelpiece, and somehow he had managed to create an ambience of cheerful business. He wore, I suppose because it was a Saturday, a sporty-looking checked shirt, and a tweed jacket, and when he looked up and smiled a welcome for me the doom-like weight that had lain in the pit of my stomach all morning was suddenly not so doom-like after all.

He stood up, and I said, "It's a gorgeous morning."

"Isn't it? Too good to be working."

"Do you always work on a Saturday?"

"Sometimes . . . depends how much there is to be done. You can get a surprising amount achieved when other people aren't ringing you up on the telephone all the time." He opened a drawer in his desk. "I changed the money for you at the current exchange rate . . . I made a note . . ."

"Don't bother about that."

"You should bother, Jane; your Scottish blood should make certain that I haven't diddled you out of a single bawbee."

"Well, if you have you can count it as personal commission." I held out my hand and he gave me a bundle of notes and some loose change. "Now you'll really be able to join the big spenders, though what you're going to find to spend it on in Caple Bridge is beyond me."

I stuffed the money in the pocket of my tinker's raincoat.

"That's what my grandmother said. She wanted to take me to Inverness, but I said I was having lunch with you."

"Do you like steaks?"

"I haven't had a steak since Father stood me dinner on my birthday. At Reef Point we lived on cold pizzas."

"How long will you be?"

"Half an hour . . ."

He looked astonished. "Is that all?"

"I loathe shopping at the best of times. Nothing ever fits, and when it does I always hate it . . . I shall come back wearing a lot of unsuitable clothes and probably in the worst of tempers."

"I shall say they're charming, and coax you back into a good mood, then." He glanced at his watch. "Half an hour . . . say, twelve? Here?"

"That's fine."

I went out again with a pocket full of money and searched for somewhere to spend it. There were butchers' shops, and grocers, and game merchants, and a gunsmith's and a garage. Eventually, between the inevitable Italian ice-cream parlour that exists in most small Scottish towns, and the Post Office, I ran Isabel McKenzie Modes to earth. Or more accurately, Isabel MODES McKenzie. I went in, through a glassed door, modestly draped in net, and found myself in a small room lined with shelves of unhopeful looking clothes. There was a glass counter filled with underclothes in peach and beige, and here and there were tastefully draped, sad, string-coloured pullovers.

My heart sank, but before I could escape, a curtain opened at the back of the shop and I was joined by a small, mouse-like woman, wearing a jersey suit two sizes too big for her, and a huge Cairngorm brooch.

"Good morning." I guessed that she had started life in Edinburgh and I wondered if she were Isabel Modes McKenzie in person, and if so, what had brought her to Caple Bridge. Perhaps she had been told that the garment trade was brisker here.

"Oh . . . good morning. I—I wanted a sweater."

As soon as I said the word I knew I had made my first mistake.

"We have some very nice *jairseys*. Did you want it in wool or bouclé?"

I said I wanted it in wool.

"And what size would it be?"

I said I supposed a sort of medium size.

She began to pull out shelves, and soon I was picking my way through sweaters in old rose, moss green and dead-leaf brown.

"H—haven't you any other colours?"

"What other colour did you have in mind?"

"Well—navy blue?"

"Oh, there's very little navy being worn this year." I wondered where she got her information. Perhaps she had a hot line to Paris.

"Now, this is a charming shade . . ."

It was petrol blue, a colour that I am convinced goes with nothing and nobody.

"I really wanted something plainer . . . you know, warm and thick . . . perhaps a polo neck . . . ?"

"Oh no, we haven't any polo necks . . . polo necks aren't be-ing . . ."

I broke in rudely, but I was getting desperate.

"It doesn't matter then, I'll leave the sweater . . . the jersey . . . Perhaps you've got some skirts?"

It started all over again. "Did you want it in tartan, or a tweed . . . ?"

"A tweed, I suppose . . ."

"And what is your waist measurement?"

Beginning to sound terse, I told her. There was more searching, this time through an unhopeful looking rack. She brought out two, and laid them, with a grand gesture, before me. One was unspeakable. The other not quite so hideous, in a brown and white herringbone. Feebly I agreed to try it on, was squeezed into a space as small as a cupboard, closed in by yet another curtain and left to get on with it. With some difficulty I struggled out of the clothes I was wearing, and pulled on the skirt. The tweed prickled, and caught at my stockings as though it had been woven from thistles. I did up the waist hooks and the zip and looked at myself in the long mirror. The effect was startling. The tweed zig-zagged around me like an op-art picture, my hips had be-come elephantine, and the waist band dug into my meagre flesh like a wire-cutter.

Isabel Modes McKenzie coughed discreetly and whisked back the curtain, like a conjurer.

"Oh, you're lovely in that," she said. "You suit tweed."

"Don't you think it's . . . well, a little bit long?"

"Skirts are longer this season you know . . ."

"Yes, but this one nearly covers my knees . . ."

"Well, if you wanted, I could take it up a fraction . . . it's very good looking . . . there's nothing so good looking as a nice tweed . . ."

To get away, I might have bought it . . . but I took another look in the mirror, and was strong-minded.

"No. No, I'm afraid it really won't do . . . it's not what I wanted." I undid the zipper and tore it off before she could talk me into buying the dreadful thing, and she took it back, sadly, averting her eyes discreetly from my petticoat.

"Perhaps you'd like to try the tartan, the ancient colours are so soft . . ."

"No . . ." I pulled on my old, American drip-dry, un-warm skirt and it felt like a friend. "No, I think I'll leave it . . . it was just an idea . . . thank you so much."

I pulled on my raincoat, picked up my bag, and together, in sidling fashion, we made for the net-curtained door. She reached it first and opened it for me, reluctantly, as though letting a prized animal out of a trap.

"Perhaps if you were passing another day . . ."

"Yes . . . maybe . . ."

"I shall be getting my new stock next week."

Straight from Dior, no doubt. "Thank you . . . I am sorry . . . good morning."

Out and away, and into the blessed open air, I turned and walked off as fast as I could. I passed the gunsmith's, and then, on an inspiration, turned round and walked back and went in, and bought, in two minutes flat, a large navy blue sweater originally intended for a young man. Relieved beyond words that my morning had not been a total failure, and clasping the sturdily wrapped parcel, I returned to David.

While he stacked papers and locked up filing cabinets, I sat on his desk and told him the saga of my disastrous shopping expedition. Spiced by his comments (he could do an Ediburgh accent to perfection) the story grew in its telling, and in the end I laughed so much that my ribs ached. We collected ourselves at last; David stuffed a pile of files into a bulging briefcase, gave a last look round, and then closed the door on his office and we went down the dingy stairs and out into the sunlit, crowded street.

He lived only a hundred yards or so from the centre of the little town, and we walked this short distance together. David's old briefcase slapped and banged against his long legs and every now and then we had to separate in order to avoid a parked perambulator or a pair of gossiping women. His house, when we came to it, was one of a row—identical, small, two-storey stone houses, each set in its own plot of ground, fronted by a modest garden, and with a gravel path leading from gate to front door. David's differed from his neighbours only in that he had added a garage, built into the space between his house and the next, with a concrete driveway connecting it to the street. And he had painted his front door a bright, sunny yellow.

He opened the gate and I followed him down the path and waited while he unlocked the door. He stood aside and waited for me to go in ahead of him. There was a narrow hallway with a staircase rising out of it, doors to right and left, and a kitchen visible through the open door at the back. It should have been very ordinary, and yet he—or somebody—had made it charming with close carpeting and leafy wallpaper, and groups of precisely arranged sporting prints.

He took my parcel and my raincoat from me, and dumped them, and his brief-case, on the chair in the hall, and then led me into a long sitting-room, with windows at either end. And it was only then that I appreciated the unique position of the unpretentious little house, for the windows to the south had been enlarged into a deep bay, and this looked out over a long narrow garden, sloping gently down towards the river.

The room itself was full of promise. Shelves of books, a stack of records, magazines on the low table in front of the fireplace. There were cushiony-looking armchairs and a little sofa, an old-fashioned cabinet filled with Meissen china, and over the mantelpiece . . . I went to look . . .

"A Ben Nicholson?" He nodded. "But not an original."

"Yes, it is. My mother gave it to me for my twenty-first."

"This reminds me of your mother's flat in London . . . it's got the same sort of feeling . . ."

"Probably because it was furnished more or less from the same house. And of course she helped me choose the curtains and the wallpaper and stuff."

Secretly glad that it was his mother, and no one else, I went over to the window. "Who would have thought you'd have a garden like this?" There was a little terrace, with a wooden table and chairs, and then a lawn, scattered now with fallen leaves, and flower-beds still filled with late roses, and clumps of purple Michaelmas daisies. There was a bird-bath and an old, leaning apple tree. "Do you do the gardening yourself?"

"You could hardly call it gardening . . . as you can see, it's not very big."

"But having the river and everything . . ."

"That's what decided me when I bought the house. I tell all my friends that I have fishing on the Caple, and they're all enormously impressed. I don't tell them that it's only ten yards . . ."

There was a clutter of photographs and snapshots arranged on the top of the bookcase, and I was irresistibly drawn to them. "Is this your mother? And your father? And you?" About twelve years old with an engaging grin. "Is this you?"

"Yes, it is."

"You didn't wear glasses then."

"I didn't wear glasses till I was sixteen."

"What happened?"

"I had an accident. It was a paper chase, at school, and the boy in front of me let a branch of a tree snap back into my eye. It wasn't his fault, it could have happened to anyone. But I partly lost the sight of the eye, and I've worn glasses ever since."

"Oh, what bad luck!"

"Not really. I can do most things I want . . . , except play tennis."

"Why can't you play tennis?"

"I don't quite know. But if I can see the ball I can't hit it, and if I can hit it, I can't see it. It doesn't make for much of a game."

We went through to the kitchen, which was as small as a galley in a yacht and so tidy that I felt ashamed at the memory of my own inadequacies. He peered into the oven where he had left some potatoes baking, and then found a frying-pan, and butter, and took a blood-stained parcel from the fridge and unfolded it to reveal a couple of inch-thick Aberdeen Angus steaks.

"Will you cook them, or shall I?" he asked.

"You cook them . . . I'll lay the table or something." I opened the door that led on to the terrace, baking in the unseasonable heat. "Can't we have lunch here? It's like being in the Mediterranean."

"If you want."

"It's blissful . . . shall we use this table?"

Talking, getting in his way, having to ask where everything was, I eventually got the table laid. While I did this, he had tossed a salad, unwrapped a crisp french loaf and taken small dishes of frosty cold butter from the refrigerator. With all this completed and the steaks gently sizzling in the pan, he poured two glasses of sherry and we went out to sit in the sunshine.

He shucked off his jacket, and leaned back, long legs stretched before him, and turned up his face to the heat.

"Tell me about yesterday," he said suddenly.

"Yesterday?"

"You walked the Lairig Ghru—" he cocked an eye at me— "or didn't you?"

"Oh. Yes, we did."

"What was it like?"

I tried to think what it had been like, and found I could remember nothing save the extraordinary discussion I had had with Sinclair after lunch.

"It was . . . all right. Marvellous, really."

"You don't sound very enthusiastic."

"Well, it was . . . marvellous." I couldn't think of any other word.

"But exhausting, perhaps."

"Yes. I was tired."

"How long did it take?"

Again, I could hardly remember. "Well, we were back by dark. Gibson met us at Loch Morlich . . ."

"Umm." He seemed to consider this. "And what's cousin Sinclair doing today?"

I stooped and picked up a piece of gravel and began to toss it, catching it on the back of my hand as though I were playing Jacks. "He's gone to London."

"To London? I thought he was on leave."

"Yes, he is." I dropped the stone, bent to pick up another. "But he had a phone call last night . . . I don't know what about . . . we found a note when we came down for breakfast this morning."

"Did he drive?"

I remembered the tiger roar of the Lotus, splitting the still darkness. "Yes, he took the car." I dropped the second stone. "He'll be back in a day or so. Monday evening, perhaps, he said." I did not want to talk about Sinclair. I was afraid of David asking questions, and, clumsily, tried to change the subject. "Do you really fish from the bottom of your garden? I shouldn't think there'd be room to cast . . . and you'd get all tied up in your apple tree . . ."

And so the conversation veered to fishing, and we talked about this, and I told him about the Clearwater river in Idaho where my father once took me for a holiday.

". . . it runs with salmon . . . you can practically lift them out with a bent pin . . ."

"You like America, don't you?"

"Yes. Yes, I do." He was silent, supine in the sunshine, and encouraged by his silence, I warmed to the subject, and the dilemma in which, inevitably, I found myself. "It's funny belonging to two countries, you never seem to quite fit into either. When I was in California I used to wish I were at Elvie. But now I'm at Elvie . . ."

"You wish you were back in California."

"Not exactly. But there are things I miss."

"Such as?"

"Well, specific things. My father, of course. And Rusty. And the sound of the Pacific, late at night, when the rollers come pouring up on to the beach."

"And what about the unspecific things?"

"That's more complicated." I tried to decide what I really missed. "Ice water. And the Bell Telephone Company. And San Francisco. And central heating. And the garden centres where you can go and buy plants and stuff and everything smells of orange blossom." I turned towards David, and found that he was watching me. Our eyes met, and he smiled. I said, "But there are good things over here too."

"Tell me about them."

"Post Offices. You can buy anything in a country Post Office— even stamps. And the way the weather is never the same, two days running. It's so much more exciting. And afternoon tea, with scones and biscuits and soggy gingerbread . . ."

"Are you reminding me in your subtle way that it's time to eat those steaks?"

"Not consciously I wasn't."

"Well, if we don't eat them now, they're not going to be eatable. Come along."

It was a perfect meal, eaten under perfect circumstances. He even opened a bottle of wine, rough and red, the exact complement to steaks and french bread, and we finished with cheese and biscuits and a bowl of fresh fruit, topped with a cluster of white grapes. I found that I was ravenous and ate enormously, wiping my plate clean with a thick white crust, and going on to peel an orange so juicy that it dripped from the ends of my fingers. When he had completely finished, David went inside to make coffee.

"Shall we have it outside?" he asked through the open door.

"Yes, let's, down by the river." I went in to join him, to run my sticky hands under a tap.

He said, "You'll find a rug in the chest in the hall. You take it down and settle yourself and I'll bring the coffee."

"What about the dishes?"

"Leave them . . . it's too good a day to waste slaving over a hot sink."

It was comfortably like the sort of remark my father would make. I went and found the rug, and took it back outside, and went down to the sloping lawn and spread the rug on the sunlit grass, only a few yards from the edge of the river. After the long dry summer, the Caple was running low, and there was a bank of pebbles, like a miniature beach, between the grass and the deep brown water.

The apple tree was loaded with fruit, windfalls lay at its feet. I went to shake it, and a few more tumbled to the grass, making soft plopping noises. Beneath the tree it was shady and cool and smelt pleasantly musty, like old lofts. I leaned against its trunk, and watched the sunlit river through a lace-work of branches. It was very peaceful.

Soothed by this, comforted by good food and easy company, I felt my spirits rise, and told myself briskly that this was a suitable moment to start being sensible about all my half-acknowledged fears. What was the point of letting them churn around at the back of my mind, nagging like a bad tooth, and giving me a perpetual stomach ache?

I would be realistic about Sinclair. There was no reason to suppose that he wouldn't accept responsibility for the baby that Tessa Faraday was going to have. When he returned to Elvie on Monday, he would probably tell us that he was going to be married, and Grandmother would be delighted (hadn't she thought the girl was charming?) and I would be delighted too, and need never say a word about the telephone call I had overheard.

And as for Gibson, he *was* getting old, there was no denying it, and perhaps it would be better for all concerned if he were to be retired. But if he did have to go, then Grandmother and Sinclair between them could surely find him a little cottage, perhaps with a garden, where he could grow vegetables, and have a few hens, and so keep himself happy and occupied.

And as for myself . . . This was not so easy to shrug off. I wished I knew why, yesterday, he had brought up the question of our getting married. Perhaps it had been simply an amusing idea to pass the half-hour after our picnic lunch. As such, I would have been prepared to accept it, but his kiss had been neither cousinly, nor light-hearted . . . just to remember it made me uncomfortable, and it was because of this that I felt so utterly confused. Perhaps he had done it deliberately, to upset me. He had always been a wicked tease. Perhaps he simply wanted to gauge my reactions . . .

"Jane."

"Um?" I turned and saw David Stewart watching me from the sunlight beyond the broken shadow of the tree. Behind him, I saw the coffee tray, set down by the rug, and I realized that he had spoken my name before, but that I had not heard. He dipped his head under the low branches and came to stand in front of me, putting up a hand to prop himself against the tree.

He said, "Is anything wrong?"

"Why do you ask that?"

"You look a little worried. You also look very pale."

"I'm always pale."

"And always worried?"

"I didn't say I was worried."

"Did . . . anything happen yesterday?"

"What do you mean?"

"Just that I noticed you weren't very anxious to talk about it."

"Nothing happened . . ." I wished I could walk off and leave him, but his arm was over my shoulder, and I couldn't get away without deliberately ducking beneath it. He turned his head to watch me from the corner of his eye, and beneath this familiar, disconcerting regard, I felt my face and neck grow warm.

"You once told me," he said pleasantly, "that when you lie, you blush. Something is wrong. . . ."

"No, it isn't. And anyway, it's nothing . . ."

"If you wanted to tell me, you would, wouldn't you? Perhaps I could help."

I thought of the girl in London, and Gibson . . . and myself, and all my fears came flooding up again. "Nobody can help," I told him. "Nobody can do anything."

He left it at that. We went back into the sunlight, and I found that I was cold, my skin crawled with goose-flesh. I sat on the warm rug and drank coffee, and David gave me a cigarette to keep the midges away. After a little, I lay down, my head on a cushion, my body spread to the sun. I was tired and the wine had made me drowsy. I closed my eyes, and the river noises took over, and presently I was asleep.

I awoke about an hour later. David lay a yard or so from me, propped on one elbow and reading a paper. I stretched and yawned, and he looked up, and I said, "This is the second time this has happened."

"What has happened?"

"I've woken, and found you there."

"I was going to wake you in a moment anyway. Wake you up and take you home."

"What time is it?"

"Half past three."

I eyed him drowsily. "Will you come back for tea at Elvie? Grandmother would love to see you."

"I would, but I have to go and see an old boy who lives out in the back of beyond. Every now and then he starts fretting about his will, and I have to go and reassure him."

"It's rather like Scottish weather, isn't it?"

"What do you mean by that?"

"One week you're in New York, doing goodness-knows-what. The next you're trailing up some remote glen to set an old man's mind at rest. Do you like being a country lawyer?"

"Yes, as a matter of fact, I do."

"You fit in so well. I mean . . . as though you'd been here all your life. And your house and everything . . . and the garden. It all goes together as though someone had matched you up."

"You match too," said David.

I longed for him to enlarge on this, and for a moment thought he was going to, but he seemed to change his mind, and instead got up, collected the coffee things and his paper and carried them back up to the house. When he returned I was still lying there, watching the river, and he stood over me, put his hands under my shoulders and pulled me to my feet. I turned and found myself in the circle of his arms, and I said, "I've done this before, too."

"Only then," said David, "your face was all swollen and blotched with crying, and today . . ."

"What about today . . ."

He laughed then. "Today you've collected about six dozen more freckles. And a lot of old apple leaves and grass in your hair."

He drove me home. The hood of his car was down, and my hair blew all over my face, and David found an old silk scarf in the cupboard on the dashboard and gave it to me, and I tied it over my head.

When we came to the roadworks, the lights were red, so we waited, the engine of the car idling, and watched the approaching traffic filing towards us down the single-line track.

"I can't help feeling," said David, "that instead of straightening out this bit of road, it would have been better to demolish the bridge and build a new one . . . or even to do something about that hellish corner on the other side."

"But the bridge is so pretty . . ."

"It's dangerous, Jane."

"But everyone knows about it, and takes it about one mile an hour."

"Not everyone knows about it," he corrected me drily. "In summer every other driver is a visitor."

The lights turned green and we moved forward, past a huge sign saying RAMP. A funny thought occurred to me. "David, you've broken the law."

"Why?"

"The notice said Ramp. And you didn't."

There was a long silence, and I thought, Oh, God, which is what I think when I've said something funny and the other person doesn't think it is.

"I don't know how to," he said at last.

"You mean you've never been taught?"

"My mother was a poor widow. She couldn't afford lessons."

"But everyone ought to be able to ramp, it's one of the social graces."

"Well," said David, easing his car over the humpbacked bridge, "for your sake, I'll make a point of learning," and with that he put down his foot, and with the wind roaring about my ears, he drove me back to Elvie.

Later, I showed my grandmother my single purchase, the navy blue sweater I had bought in the gunsmith's.

"I think," she said, "you were very clever to find anything at all in Caple Bridge. And it certainly looks very warm," she added kindly, eyeing the shapeless garment. "What will you wear it with?"

"Pants . . . anything. I really wanted a skirt, but I couldn't find anything."

"What sort of a skirt?"

"Something warm . . . perhaps next time you go to Inverness . . ."

"What about a kilt?" said my grandmother.

I had not thought of this. It seemed a splendid idea. Kilts are the cosiest things in the world, and the colours are always mouth-melting. "Where could I buy a kilt?"

"Oh, my dear, you don't need to buy one, the house is full of them. Sinclair's worn kilts since he could walk and not one has ever been thrown away."

I had forgotten the happy fact that a kilt, unlike a bicycle, is sexless. "But that's a marvellous idea! Why didn't we think of it before? I'll go and look right away. Where are they? In the attic?"

"Not at all. They're in Sinclair's room, in the cupboard on top of his wardrobe. I packed them all away in moth balls, but if you do want one, we can hang it out to air, and get rid of the smell, and it'll be as good as new."

Not wanting to waste a moment, I went in search of a kilt. Sinclair's room, for the moment vacant of its owner, had been cleaned and swept, and was immaculately tidy. I remembered this inherent neatness had always been strong in his character. As a boy he could not stand disorder, and never had to have his clothes folded, or his toys put away.

I took up a chair and went across to his cupboard. This had been built in to the alcove at the side of the fireplace, and the space above the top of the wardrobe was put to use as extra cupboard space for suitcases and out-of-season clothes. I stood on the chair and opened the doors, and saw a neat stack of books, some motoring magazines, a squash racket, a pair of swimming flippers. There was a strong smell of camphor coming from a huge dress box, all laced up with string, and I reached up to lift this down. It was heavy and awkward, and as I struggled with it, my elbow caught the pile of books, and dislodged them. Encumbered as I was, there was nothing I could do to stop them falling, and simply stood on the chair and listened to them crashing, in terrible disorder, to the floor.

I swore, took a firmer grip of my burden, lifted it down, laid it on the bed, and stooped to retrieve the books. They were mostly text books, a Thesaurus, *Le Petite Larousse*, a life of Michaelangelo, and, at the bottom . . .

It was thick and heavy, bound in scarlet leather, the cover emblazoned with a private coat-of-arms, the title tooled in gold letters on the crimson spine, *A History of the Earth and Animated Nature*, Volumes I and II.

I knew that book. I was six years old again, and my father had brought it back to Elvie after one of his spasmodic forays into Mr. McFee's second-hand book shop in Caple Bridge. Mr. McFee had died a long time ago, and the shop was now a tobacconist's, but in those days my father had spent many happy hours discoursing with Mr. Mc-Fee, a cheerful eccentric with no tiresome prejudices about dirt or dust, and browsing through endless shelves of musty volumes.

He had found Goldsmith's *Animated Nature* by chance, and brought it home in triumph, for not only was it a rare volume, but it had been privately bound by some previous noble owner, and was, in itself, a thing of beauty. Delighted with it, wanting to share his pleasure, the first thing my father did was to bring it up to the nursery to show to Sinclair and myself. My reaction was probably disappointing. I stroked the pretty leather, looked at one or two pictures of Asian elephants, and then returned to my jigsaw puzzle.

But with Sinclair it was different. Sinclair loved everything about it, the old printing, the thick pages, the aquatints, the detail of the tiny drawings. He loved the smell, and the marbled endpapers, and the very weight of the big old book.

The addition of such a prize to my father's collection seemed to merit some sort of ceremony. Accordingly, he went off to fetch one of his own Ex Libris labels, a woodcut, with his initial wound about with much decorative plant life, and solemnly affixed it to the marbled endpaper of Goldsmith's *Animated Nature*. Sinclair and I watched this operation in total silence, and when it was done I heaved a sigh of satisfaction, because it had been accomplished so neatly, and because it proved, beyond any shadow of doubt, that the book now belonged to my father.

It was then taken downstairs and left on a table in the drawing-room, along with some magazines and daily newspapers, where it could be admired, and handled, and perused in passing. It was not spoken of again until two or three days later when my father realized that it had disappeared.

No one was particularly concerned, Goldsmith's *Animated Nature* had simply been moved. Someone had borrowed it, perhaps, forgotten to put it back. But no one had. My father began to ask questions, and drew nothing but blanks. My grandmother searched diligently, but the book did not come to light.

Sinclair and I were then involved. Had we seen the book? But of course we hadn't, and said so, and our innocence was never questioned. My mother started to say: "Perhaps a burglar . . ." but my grandmother pooh-poohed this. What burglar would turn a blind eye to the Georgian silver and make off with only an old book? She insisted that Goldsmith's *Animated Nature* was simply mislaid. It would turn up. Like any nine-day wonder the mysterious affair died a natural death, but the book was never found.

Until now. In Sinclair's cupboard, neatly filed away with some other possessions for which he did not have a regular use. And it was as beautiful as ever, the red leather smooth and soft to touch, the lettering bright and gold. Standing with it, heavy as lead in my hands, I remembered Father's Ex Libris, and I lifted the front cover of the book, and saw that the marble endpaper and the Ex Libris had been removed altogether, delicately and finely, close to the spine, probably with a razor blade. And on the white fly-leaf which lay below was written in Sinclair's firm, black, twelve-year-old writing:

Sinclair Bailey,
Elvie.
THIS IS HIS BOOK

Chapter 9

THE BEAUTIFUL, FINE WEATHER went on. On the Monday afternoon, my grandmother, armed with a spade and a pair of gardening gloves, went out to plant bulbs. I offered to help her, but she declined. If I was there, we would only talk, she said, and nothing would get done. She would be quicker on her own. Thus rejected, I whistled up the dogs and set off for a walk. I don't much like gardening anyway.

I went for miles and was out for two hours or more. By the time I returned, the brightness of the day was beginning to fade, and it was turning cold. A few clouds had appeared over the tops of the mountains, blown from the north, and a drift of mist lay over the loch. From the walled garden, where Will was stoking a bonfire, plumed a long feather of blue smoke, and the air was filled with the smell of burning rubbish. With my hands deep in my pockets, and my head full of thoughts of tea by the fire, I crossed the causeway and came up the road beneath the copper beeches. One of the dogs began to bark, and I looked up, and saw, parked in front of the house, the dark yellow Lotus Elan.

Sinclair was back. I looked at my watch. Five o'clock. He was early. I went on, across the grass, ankle-deep in fallen leaves, on to the gravel. As I passed the car, I trailed my hand across one glossy bumper, as if to reassure myself that it was really there. I went into the warm, peat-smelling hall, waited for the dogs, and then shut the door behind me.

I heard the murmur of voices from the drawing-room. The dogs went to drink from their bowl and then collapsed in front of the hall fire. I unbuckled the belt of my raincoat, and pulled it off, toed off my muddied shoes, smoothed my hair down with my hands. I crossed the hall and opened the door. I said, "Hello, Sinclair."

They had been sitting on either side of the fire, with a low tea table between them. But now Sinclair got up and came across the room to greet me.

"Janey . . . where have you been?" He kissed me.

"For a walk."

"It's nearly dark, we thought you'd got lost."

I looked up at him. I had thought that he would be noticeably different. Quieter; tired, perhaps, from his long drive. More thoughtful, weighed down with new responsibilities. But it was obvious that I had thought wrong. If anything, he looked gayer, younger and more lighthearted than ever. There was a glitter to him that evening—a shine of excitement, like a child on Christmas Eve.

He took my hands. "And you're as cold as ice. Come on over by the fire and get warm. I've kindly left you one piece of toast, but I'm sure if you want some more Mrs Lumley will make it."

"No, that's fine." I pulled up a low leather stool and sat between them, and my grandmother poured my tea. "Where did you go?" she asked, and I told her. "Have the dogs had a drink? Were they wet and muddy? Did you dry them?" I assured her that they had, they weren't, and I hadn't needed to. "We didn't go anywhere wet, and I picked up all the heather off their coats before we got home." She handed me the cup and I folded my cold hands round it, and looked at Sinclair.

"How was London?"

"Hot and stuffy." He grinned, his eyes glinting with amusement. "Full of exhausted businessmen in winter suits."

"Did you . . . achieve what you went to do?"

"That sounds very pompous. Achieve. Where did you learn a long word like that?"

"Well, did you?"

"Yes, of course I did, I wouldn't be here otherwise."

"When—when did you leave London?"

"Early this morning . . . about six o'clock . . . Grandmother, is there any more tea in that pot?"

She lifted the teapot, took off the lid to look. "Not really. I'll go and make some more."

"Get Mrs Lumley . . ."

"No, her feet are hurting, I'll make it. I want to talk to her about dinner anyway, we'll need to put another pheasant in the casserole."

When she had gone, "Delicious, pheasant casserole," said Sinclair, and he took my wrist in his fingers, ringing it, like a bracelet, with his fingers. His touch was cool and light. He said, "I want to talk to you."

This was it. "What about?"

"Not here, I want you all to myself. I thought after tea we'd go out in the car. Up to the top of Bengairn and watch the moon rise. Will you come?"

If he wanted to tell me privately about Tessa, I supposed that the inside of the Lotus Elan was as good a place as any. I said, "All right."

Driving in the Lotus was, for me, a new experience. Lashed low into the seat by the band of my seat belt, I felt as if I was on my way to the moon, and the speed with which Sinclair took off did nothing to dispel this impression. We roared up the lane, paused for a moment at the main road, and then streamed out and on to it, the needle of the speedometer climbing to seventy in a matter of seconds, and fields and hedges and familiar landmarks flying up and falling away in dizzying succession.

I said, "Do you always drive so fast?"

"Darling, this isn't fast."

I left it at that. In no time it seemed, we were at the hump-backed bridge, slowed slightly, and then swept over it—leaving my stomach suspended somewhere two feet over my head—and poured down towards the roadworks. The lights were green, and Sinclair accelerated, so that we were through the obstruction and well beyond before they changed back to red.

We came to Caple Bridge and the thirty-mile limit. In deference to the local police constable, and much to my relief, he changed down, and idled the Lotus through the town at the regulation speed, but once the last house had dropped behind, we were off again. Now, there was no traffic. The road, smoothly cambered, curved ahead of us, and the car leapt forward, like a horse given its head.

We came to our turning, the small side road that led to the south, climbing in a succession of steep bends, up to and over the summit of Bengairn. Fields and the farmland dropped below us; with a roar of tyres we crossed the cattle grid, and were now on the moor, the blown grass patched with heather, and populated only by mildly interested flocks of black-faced sheep. The cold air, blown through the open window, smelt of peat, and there was mist ahead of us, but before we had driven into this, Sinclair turned the Lotus into a lay-by, and switched off the engine.

The view spread before us, the valley quiet beneath a sky of pale turquoise, more green than blue, and washed, in the west, with the pink of sunset. Far below, Elvie Loch lay still and bright as a jewel, and the Caple was a winding silver ribbon. It was very quiet; only the wind nudging at the car, and the cry of curlews.

Beside me, Sinclair undid his seat belt, and then, when I did not move to follow his example, leaned over to undo mine. I turned then, to look at him, and without saying anything, he took my face between his gloved hands and kissed me. After a little, I pushed him gently away. I said, "You wanted to talk to me, remember?"

He smiled, not in the least put out, and heaved himself around in order to reach a pocket. "I've got something for you . . ." He took out a small box and opened it, and it seemed that all the sky was reflected in the star-sparkle of diamonds.

I felt as though I was rolling, somersaulting, topsy-turvy down a long, steep bank. I came out of it reeling and stupid. When I could speak, I could only say, "But Sinclair, that's not for *me*."

"Of course it is. Here . . ." He took out the ring, tossed the little box casually on to the shelf on the dashboard, and before I could stop him had taken my left hand and thrust the ring deep on to my finger. I tried to pull away, but he held on to my hand, and closed it, clenched round the ring, so that the diamonds bit into my flesh and hurt.

"But it *can't* be for me . . ."

"Just for you. Only for you."

"Sinclair, we have to talk."

"That's why I brought you here."

"No, not about this. About Tessa Faraday."

If I had thought this would shock him, I was mistaken. "What do you know about Tessa Faraday?" He sounded indulgent, not in the least upset.

"I know that she's going to have a baby. Your baby."

"And how did you find that out?"

"Because the night she rang up, I heard the telephone and I went to answer it, on the upstairs extension. But you'd answered it already, and I heard her . . . telling you . . ."

"So it was you?" He sounded quite relieved as though some small dilemma had been solved. "I thought I heard the other line cut off. How very tactful of you not to listen to the end of the conversation."

"But what are you going to do about it?"

"Do? Nothing."

"But that girl is having your baby."

"Darling Janey, we don't know that it is my baby."

"But it *could* be yours."

"Oh, yes, it could be. But that doesn't mean that it is. And I am not taking the responsibility for another man's carelessness."

I thought of Tessa Faraday and the image I had built up of her. The gay and pretty girl, held, laughing, in the curve of Sinclair's arm. The successful, dedicated ski-er, with her own chosen world at her feet. The young woman, approved and admired, lunching at the Connaught with my grandmother. "Such a charming girl" my grandmother had said, and she was seldom mistaken about people. None of this had anything to do with the impression that Sinclair was trying to give me.

I said, carefully, "Did you tell her that?"

"In so many words, yes."

"What did she say?"

He shrugged slightly. "She said if that was how I felt, she would make other arrangements."

"And you left it at that?"

"Yes. We left it at that. Don't be too naïve, Jane, she's been around, she's a sensible girl." All this time, he had not loosened his grip on my arm, but now he let it go, and I was able to unfold and stretch my cramped fingers, and he took hold of the ring between his forefinger and thumb, and turned it a little, to and fro, as though he were screwing it on. "Anyway," he said, "I told her that I was going to marry you."

"You told her *what?*"

"Oh, darling, do listen. I told her I was going to marry you . . ."

"But you had no right to do that . . . you haven't even asked me."

"Of course I've asked you. What did you think we were discussing the other day? What did you think I was doing?"

"Play acting."

"Well—I wasn't. And, what's more, you know I wasn't."

"You're not in love with me."

"But I love you." He made it sound entirely reasonable. "And being with you, and having you back at Elvie, is the best thing that's ever happened to me. There's such a freshness about you, Janey. One moment you're as naïve as a child, and the next, you come out with something so astonishingly wise. And you make me laugh; and I find you deliciously attractive. And you know me almost better than I know myself. Isn't all that better than simply being in love?"

I said, "But if you marry someone, it's for ever."

"Well?"

"You must have been in love with Tessa Faraday, and now you don't want anything more to do with her . . ."

"Janey, that was entirely different."

"How different? I don't see how it's so different."

"Tessa's attractive and gay and very easy to be with, and I enjoyed her company enormously . . . but for a lifetime . . . no."

"She's going to have that child for the rest of her life."

"I've already told you, it almost certainly isn't mine."

It was obvious that from that angle he considered himself invulnerable. I tried another tack. "Supposing, Sinclair, just supposing, that I didn't want to marry you. Like I said the other day, we're first cousins . . ."

"It's happened before . . ."

"We're too close . . . I wouldn't want to risk it."

"I love you," said Sinclair. It was the first time anyone had ever said that to me. I had often imagined it happening in secret teenage day-dreams. But never like this.

"But . . . but I don't love you . . ."

He smiled. "You don't sound very sure."

"But I am. Quite sure."

"Not even enough to . . . help me?"

"Oh, Sinclair, you don't need help."

"But that's where you're wrong. I do. If you don't marry me, then my world will come crashing in little pieces around my ears."

It was a lover-like statement, and yet I did not believe it was said with love.

"You mean that literally, don't you?"

"How perceptive you can be, Janey. Yes, I do."

"Why?"

He was suddenly impatient, dropping my hand as though he were bored with it, turning for diversion to search for a cigarette. There were some in his coat pocket. He took one, and lit it from the lighter on the dashboard. "Oh, because," he said at last.

After a little, "Because?" I prompted him.

He took a deep breath. "Because I'm over my ears in debt. Because I have either to find the money to pay it, or the security to borrow and I haven't got either. And if it all comes out, which it's in deadly danger of doing, then I have every certainty that my managing director will send for me and reluctantly inform me that he can do very nicely without my services, thank you."

"You mean, you'll lose your job?"

"Not only perceptive, but also quick on the uptake."

"But . . . how did you get into debt?"

"How do you think? Backing horses, playing blackjack . . ."

It sounded very harmless. "But how much for?"

He told me. I couldn't believe anyone could have so much money, let alone owe it. "You must be out of your mind. You mean, just playing cards . . ."

"Oh, for heaven's sake, Jane, you can lose that much in some gambling clubs in London in a single evening. And it's taken me the best part of two years."

It took me a moment or two to accept the fact that any man could be such a fool. I had always thought my father was completely unrealistic about money, but this . . .

"Couldn't Grandmother help you? Lend you the money?"

"She's helped me before . . . without obvious enthusiasm, I may add."

"You mean, this isn't the first time."

"No, it isn't the first time, and you can take off that shocked, pie-faced expression. Besides, our grandmother doesn't have that much money lying around. She belongs to a generation that believes in tying up her capital, and hers is all in trusts and investments and land."

Land. I said, casually, "How about selling some land, then? The . . . moor, for instance?"

Sinclair sent me a sideways glance, full of reluctant respect. "I'd already thought of that. I'd even lined up a group of Americans more than anxious to buy the moor, or if they couldn't do that, then to take it yearly at a substantial rent. To be honest, Janey, that's why I took this bit of leave, to come north and put the idea to her. But of course, she won't think of it . . . though what possible good it can be to her as it is, is more than I can imagine."

"It's rented out already . . ."

"For peanuts. The rent that little syndicate pays her scarcely covers the cost of Gibson's cartridges."

"And Gibson?"

"Oh, to hell with Gibson. He's past it anyway, it's time he was pensioned off."

We fell silent once more. Sinclair sat smoking, and I, beside him, tried frantically to sort out a confusion of thoughts. I found that what astonished me was not his soulless attitude—I had already suspected this—nor the fact that he had got himself into such a mess; but simply that he had been so frank with me. Either he had given up all idea of our getting married, and so had nothing to lose, or else his conceit of himself was without bounds.

I was beginning to be angry. I lose my temper slowly and seldom, but once I do I become quite incoherent. Knowing this, and anxious for it not to happen, I deliberately battened down my finer feelings, and concentrated on staying cool and practical.

"I don't really see why it should be my grandmother's decision any more than yours. After all, Elvie will belong to you one day. If you want to sell off great chunks of it now, I should think that that would be your concern."

"What makes you say that Elvie will belong to me?"

"Of course it will. You're her grandson. There isn't anyone else."

"You talk as though it were entailed, as though it had come down through generations, from father to son. But it isn't. It hasn't. It belongs to our grandmother, and if she chooses, she can leave it to a cats' home."

"But why not you?"

"Because, my darling, I am my father's son."

"And what is that meant to mean?"

"It means that I am a no-good, a ne'er-do-well, a black sheep. A true Bailey, if you like." I stared at him blankly, and suddenly he laughed and it was not a pleasant sound. "Didn't anyone ever tell you, little innocent Jane, about your Uncle Aylwyn? Didn't your father tell you?"

I shook my head.

"I was told when I was eighteen . . . as a sort of unwanted birthday present. You see, Aylwyn Bailey was not merely dishonest, but incompetent as well. Five of those years he spent in Canada, he spent in jail. For fraud and embezzlement and God knows what else. Didn't it ever occur to you that the whole set-up was a little unnatural? No visits. Very few letters. And not a single photograph in the whole of the house?"

It was suddenly so obvious that I wondered why I had never realized the truth for myself. And I thought of the conversation I had had with my grandmother, only days ago, and the tiny glimpses she had let me have of her only son. *He chose to live in Canada, and finally to die there. Elvie never meant very much to Aylwyn . . . He looked like Sinclair. And he was very charming.*

I said, stupidly, "But why did he never come back?"

"I suppose he was a sort of remittance man . . . probably our grandmother imagined that I would be better off without his influence." He pressed the button that lowered his window, and tossed away the half-smoked cigarette. "But the way things turned out, I don't suppose it made any difference, one way or the other. I've simply inherited the family disease." He smiled at me. "And what can't be cured must be endured."

"You mean everyone else has to do the enduring."

"Oh, come, it's not easy for me either. You know, Janey, it's odd that you should bring that up—about Elvie eventually coming to me, because the other night, when we were discussing selling the moor and what to do about Gibson, that was my final ace, the one I'd kept tucked up my sleeve. "Elvie will be mine one day. Sooner or later it will be mine. So why shouldn't I decide now what is to be done with it?" He turned to me and smiled . . . his charming, disarming smile. "And do you know what our grandmother said?"

"No."

"She said, 'But, Sinclair, that's where you are mistaken. Elvie means nothing to you except as a source of income. You've made a life for yourself in London and you would never want to live here. Elvie will go to Jane.'"

And so this was how I came into it. This was the final piece of the jigsaw and now the picture was complete.

"So that's why you want to marry me. To get your hands on Elvie."

"It sounds a little bald put that way . . ."

"*Bald!*"

". . . but I suppose you could say that that was the rough idea. On top of all the other reasons I have already given you. Which are real and true and entirely sincere."

It was his use of those words which finally tipped my temper over the bounds of control, like a boulder sent rolling down a hill.

"Real and true and sincere. Sinclair, you don't even know the

meaning of those words, and how you can use them, in the same breath
. . . as telling me all this . . ."

"You mean about my father?"

"No, I don't mean about your father. I don't give a damn about
your father and neither should you. And I don't give a damn about
Elvie. I don't even want Elvie, and if Grandmother leaves it to me, I
shall refuse it, burn it down, give it away, rather than let you get your
greedy hands on it."

"That's not very charitable."

"I don't mean it to be charitable. You don't merit charity. You're
obsessed by possessions, you always have been. You always had to *have*
things . . . and if you didn't have them, you simply took them. Electric trains, and boats, and cricket bats and guns when you were small.
And now fancy cars, and flats in London and money and money and
more money. You'd never be satisfied. Even if I did everything you
wanted me to, married you and handed Elvie over, lock, stock and
barrel, that wouldn't be enough . . ."

"You're being unrealistic."

"I don't call it that. That's not what it's called. It's simply a question of getting your priorities right and knowing that people matter
more than things."

"People?"

"Yes, people. You know, human beings, with feelings and emotions and all the things you seem to have forgotten about, if you ever
knew they existed. People like our grandmother, and Gibson, and that
girl Tessa, having your baby . . . and don't start telling me that it isn't
your child, because I know, and what is more, you know damn well
that it is. They've served their purpose and they're expendable, and so
you simply push them overboard."

"Not you," said Sinclair. "I'm not pushing you. I'm taking you
with me."

"Oh, no you're not." The ring was too tight. I dragged it off,
bruising my knuckle, and just managed to resist throwing it in his face.
I reached for the little jeweller's box, jammed the ring back into the
velvet, snapped the box shut, and tossed it back on to the shelf. "You
were right when you said we loved each other. We did, and I always
thought you were the most wonderful person in the world. But you've
turned out to be not only despicable, but stupid as well. You must be
out of your mind to imagine that I would simply play along with you as

though nothing had happened. You must think that I am the most terrible fool."

To my horror I heard my voice start to shake. I flung myself away from him, and sat trembling, longing to be out in the open, or in some enormous room where I could scream and throw things around and generally indulge in a fit of hysterics. But I wasn't. I was pinned into the tiny space of Sinclair's car, and there was scarcely room in it for our seething emotions, let alone us.

Beside me, I heard him sigh. He said, "Who would have thought you'd return from America with such a set of lofty principles."

"It has nothing to do with America. It's just the way I am and the way I'll always be." I could feel my mouth go down, my eyes fill with tears. "And now I want to go home."

It wasn't any good. Despite my efforts, I started to cry in earnest. I searched for a handkerchief, but of course couldn't find one, and eventually had to accept Sinclair's which, silently, he handed me.

I wiped my eyes and blew my nose, and for some ridiculous reason this mundane action broke the tension between us. He took a couple of cigarettes from his pocket and lit them both and gave me one. Life went on. I noticed that while we talked the light had faded. The moon, not new any more, but still curved and delicate, was rising in the east, but its clarity was blurred by the mist which had dropped from the top of the mountain, and now enveloped us.

I blew my nose again. I said, "What will you do?"

"God knows."

"Perhaps if we spoke to David Stewart . . ."

"No."

"Or my father. He may not be very practical, but he's very wise. We could call him . . ."

"No."

"But, Sinclair . . ."

"You were right," he said. "It's time to go home." He put out a hand to switch on the ignition. The engine purred into life, drowning all other sounds. "But we'll stop off for a drink in Caple Bridge on the way. I think we both need one—I certainly do, and it'll give your face time to recover before Grandmother sees it."

"What's wrong with my face?"

"It's all puffy and swollen. Just like when you had the measles. It makes you look like a little girl again."

Chapter 10

THE SERIOUS BUSINESS of drinking in Scotland is, like going to funerals, a purely male prerogative. Females of any sort are not welcomed in the public bars, and if a man should make the mistake of taking his wife or girl-friend into a pub, he is expected to do his entertaining in some dim parlour, well out of sight and sound of the rest of his roistering cronies.

The Crimond Arms in Caple Bridge was no exception to this rule. We were shown that evening into a chill and unwelcoming room, papered in orange, furnished with cane chairs and tables, and decorated with flights of plaster ducks and the occasional vase of dusty plastic flowers. There was a gas fire, unlit, some large brewery ashtrays, and an upright piano which, on inspection, proved to be firmly locked. We were defied to enjoy ourselves.

Depressed and chilled by the room, by nameless fears for Sinclair, by everything that had happened, I sat alone, waiting for him. He came at last, bearing a small pale sherry for me, and a large dark whisky for himself. He said at once, "Why haven't you lit the fire?"

Thinking of the locked piano and the general air of disapproving unwelcome, I said, "I didn't think I'd be allowed to."

"You're ridiculous," said Sinclair, and took a match and knelt to light the gas fire. There was a small explosion, a strong smell, and a blaze of little flames, and a ray of heat was impinged upon a minute area around my knees.

"Is that better?"

It wasn't, for my chill seeped from deep inside me, and couldn't be warmed away, but I said that it was. Satisfied, he sat himself in a little cane chair which stood across the fancy hearth-rug, found a cigarette and lit it, and raised his whisky glass in my general direction.

"I looks towards you," he said.

It was an old joke, and as such, recognizable as a flag of truce. I was meant to say, "And I raises my glass," but I didn't because I was not sure if I could ever be friends with him again.

After that, he did not speak again. I finished my sherry, put down my empty glass, and seeing that he was only half-way through his, said that I would go and find a Ladies, with the idea of checking on my general appearance before facing up to my grandmother. Sinclair said that he would wait, so I went out and stumbled down a passage and up a flight of stairs and found the Ladies, which was no more welcoming or prepossessing than the dismal room downstairs. I looked in the mirror and was met by a dejected reflection, my face blotchy and swollen, and my mascara smudged. I washed my hands and face in cold water, and found a comb in my pocket and smoothed the tangles out of my hair, and all the time felt as though I were dressing a dead body, like those macabre stories about American morticians.

All this took some time, and when I went back downstairs again, I found the cheerless room empty, but heard, from behind the door which led into the bar proper, the sound of Sinclair's voice, talking to the barman, and guessed that he had grabbed the opportunity of buying himself the other half and drinking it under more congenial circumstances.

Not wanting to hang around, I went out to the car to wait for him. It had begun to rain, and the market place was wet and black as a lake, shimmering with the orange reflections of the street lights. I sat huddled and cold, lacking even the energy to find and light a cigarette, and presently I saw the door of the Crimond Arms open, Sinclair's silhouette showed black for a moment, and then the door fell shut, and he came across the wetness towards me.

He was carrying a newspaper.

He got into the Lotus, behind the wheel, slammed the door, and simply sat there, breathing. There was a smell of whisky, and I found myself wondering just how many whiskies he had found time to drink while I was upstairs washing my face. After a little, when he still made no move to start the car, I said, "Is anything wrong?"

He did not reply. He simply sat, looking down, his profile pale, his lashes lying dark and thick against the bones of his cheek.

I was suddenly concerned. "Sinclair."

He handed me the paper. I saw that it was the local evening news, which he had, presumably, picked up off the bar. By the light of the street lamps, I read the headlines which told of a bus accident; there was a photograph of a newly-elected town councillor, a column on some Thrumbo girl who had made good in New Zealand . . .

And then I found it, an inch of type, down in the bottom corner.

DEATH OF WELL-KNOWN SKIER
The body of Miss Tessa Faraday was found yesterday morning in her home at Crawley Court, London, S.W.1. Miss Faraday, who was 22, was the winner of the Ladies' Ski Championship held last winter . . .

The print danced and swam and was lost. I closed my eyes, as though to shut the horror away, but the darkness only made it worse and I knew that there could be no escape from the inside of my own head. *She said she would make other arrangements*, Sinclair had told me. *She's been around. She's a sensible girl.*

I said, stupidly, "But she's killed herself . . ."

I opened my eyes. He had not moved. I heard my own voice, saying, "Did you know what the other arrangements were going to be?"

He said, dully, "I thought she meant she'd get rid of it."

I was suddenly very wise. I knew. I said, "She wouldn't have been afraid of having the baby. She wasn't that sort of a girl. She killed herself because she knew you didn't love her any longer. You were going to marry someone else."

He suddenly rounded on me savagely in a storm of rage. "Shut up, and don't say anything about her, do you hear? Don't speak about her, talk about her, say one single, solitary word. You don't know anything about her, so don't pretend to. You don't understand, and you could never be expected to."

And with that, he switched on the ignition, let off the brake, and with a great swish of wet tyres on wet cobbles, swung the Lotus round, across the square, and in the direction of the street that led out into the country, and so to Elvie.

He was drunk, or frightened, or heartbroken, or shocked. Or perhaps all of these things. There was no thought now of rules or regulations or even simple native caution. Sinclair was escaping, hounded by a thousand devils, and speed was his only defence.

107

We roared through the narrow streets of the little town, and rocketed out into the dark country beyond. Reality became nothing but the road ahead, the white lines and cats' eyes at its centre pouring headlong towards us so that they were all blurred into a single entity. I had never before been really physically frightened, but now I found my teeth were clenched until they ached, and my foot pressed down so hard upon an imaginary brake that I was in real danger of dislocating my spine. We came around the last corner, and the way lay clear to the roadworks. The light was green, and in order to get through before it changed colour, he gave the Lotus more power, and we surged forward, faster than ever. I found myself praying, *Let the light go red. Now. Please let the light go red.*

And then, with only fifty yards or so to go, the miracle happened, and the light did go red. Sinclair started to brake, and I knew in that moment what I should do. To the tearing of tyres the Lotus finally jarred to a stop, and, shaking all over, I opened the door on my side, and got out.

He said, "What are you doing?"

I stood in the rain and the darkness, caught like a moth in the beam of slowly approaching headlights, as the traffic from the other direction moved towards us.

"I'm frightened," I told him.

He said, quite kindly, "Get back in. You'll get wet."

"I'll walk."

"But it's four miles . . ."

"I want to walk."

"Janey . . ." He leaned across as though to pull me back into the car, but I stepped back out of his reach.

"Why?" he asked.

"I told you, I'm frightened. And the light's gone green again . . . you must go or you'll hold everybody up."

To add conviction to my words, a small van, drawn in behind Sinclair, blew its horn. It made a rude and impudent noise, the sort of noise, which, in other times, and other places, would have made us laugh.

He said at last, "All right." He took hold of the door handle to pull it shut, and then hesitated.

"You were right about one thing, Janey," he said.

"What was that?"

"That baby of Tessa's. It *was* mine."

I began to cry. Tears mingled with the rain on my face and I could do nothing to stop them, could think of nothing to say, no way of helping him. Then the door slammed shut between us, and the next moment he was gone, the car moving away from me through the obstructions and the flashing lights, faster and faster towards the bridge.

Like a nightmare, for no reason, I found that my head was full of music, jangling like a barrel organ, and it was Sinclair's tune, and now that it was too late, I wished that I had gone with him.

"Step we gaily, on we go,
Heel for heel and toe for toe
Arm in arm, and row on row . . ."

He had reached the bridge now, and the Lotus took its soaring hump-back like a steeplechaser. The tail light disappeared over the edge of the curve and the next moment the still night was torn with the scream of brakes, of tyres skidding on wet tarmac. And then the crunch of shattered metal, a spatter of broken glass. I began to run, as useless as a person in a dream, stumbling and splashing through the puddles, surrounded by flashing lights and great red cats' eyes spelling out DANGER, but before I had got within a hundred yards of the bridge, there came the soft thud of an explosion, and, before my eyes, the whole night flowered into the rosy glow of flamelight.

It was not until after Sinclair's funeral that I had the chance to talk to my grandmother. Before that, any sort of conversation had been impossible. We were both shocked and instinctively shied from the mention of his name, as though even to talk about him would open the flood-gates of our carefully controlled grief. To add to this, there was so much to do, so much to arrange and so many people to see. Especially so many people to see. Old friends, like the Gibsons, and Will the gardener, the Minister, and Jamie Drysdale, the Thrumbo joiner, transformed by sober clothes and a suitable expression of pious gloom, into an undertaker. There were interviews with the police, and telephone calls from the press. There were flowers, and letters, dozens of letters. We started to reply to them, but finally gave up, leaving them to pile up on the brass tray in the hall.

My grandmother, belonging to a generation that is not afraid of the idea of death, and so is undistressed by its trappings, had insisted on a proper, old-fashioned funeral, and had come through it without visible tremor, even when Hamish Gibson, on leave from his regiment, played "The Flowers of the Forest" on his pipes. She had sung the hymns in church, stood, for half an hour or more, shaking hands; remembered to thank even those who had performed the most humble tasks.

But now she was tired. Mrs Lumley, exhausted with emotion and standing, had returned to her room to put up her swollen feet, so after I had lit the drawing-room fire, I settled my grandmother beside it, and went into the kitchen to make a cup of tea.

Standing against the warmth of the Aga, waiting for the kettle to boil, I stared absently out of the window at the grey world beyond. It was October now, the afternoon cold and quite motionless. Not a breath of wind stirred the last few remaining leaves from the trees. The loch, reflecting the grey sky, was still as a sheet of silver, the hills beyond bloomed softly, like plums. Tomorrow, perhaps, or the day after, they would be frosted with the first snows—it was cold enough for that—and we would be into winter.

The kettle boiled, so I made the tea, and carried it back to the drawing-room, and the chink of teacups and the crackle of the fire were comforting, as small things always are in the face of tragedy.

My grandmother was knitting a child's woollen hat in scarlet and white, destined, I knew, for the Church Christmas bazaar. Thinking that she wanted to be quiet, I had set down my empty teacup, lit a cigarette and was reading the paper, half-lost in a review of a new play, when she suddenly spoke.

"I've been feeling very guilty, Jane. I should have told you about Aylwyn, that day when we were sitting out in the garden, and you started to ask me about him. I was on the verge of doing so, and then something made me change my mind. It was very stupid of me."

I had lowered the paper, and now folded it. Her needles clicked gently on, she had not looked up from her knitting.

I said, "Sinclair told me . . ."

"Did he? I thought perhaps he would. It mattered very much to Sinclair. It would be important to him that you should know. Were you very shocked?"

"Why should I be shocked?"

"For a number of reasons. Because he was dishonest. Because he went to prison. Because I tried to hide it from you all."

"It was probably better hidden. It would have done us no good to know. Nor him."

"I always thought perhaps your father would have told you."

"No."

"That was good of him . . . he knew how fond you were of Sinclair."

I put the newspaper down and lowered myself on to the hearthrug—a good place for confidences. "But why was Aylwyn *like* that? Why wasn't he like you?"

"He was a Bailey," said my grandmother simply. "And a feckless lot they've always been, but with all the charm in the world. Not a penny to bless themselves with, and less idea of earning money or holding on to it than the man in the moon."

"Was your husband like that?"

"Oh, yes." She smiled to herself as though remembering a long-ago joke. "Do you know the first thing that happened after we were married? My father paid off all his debts. But it didn't take him long to acquire some new ones."

"Did you love him?"

"Madly. But I very soon learned that I'd married an irresponsible boy without the slightest intention of reforming."

"But you were happy."

"He died so soon after we were married, I didn't have time to be anything else. But I realized then that I was on my own, and I decided that it would be better for my children if I made an entirely new start, away from the Baileys. So I bought Elvie, and I brought my children here. I thought everything would be different. But you know, environment doesn't entirely cancel out heredity, whatever child psychologists may say. I told you about Aylwyn. I watched him grow up, and turn into his father all over again, and there wasn't a thing I could do to stop him. He grew up and he went to London and he got a job, but in no time at all he was in a financial mess. I helped him, of course, over and over again, but the day inevitably came when I couldn't help. He'd manipulated some shares, or taken some sort of fraudulent action, and the head of his firm said, quite rightly, that it was a matter for the police. But in the end I persuaded him otherwise, and he agreed to say nothing, provided Aylwyn gave his word never to practise in the City of London again. So that's why he went to Canada. But of course, the whole business simply repeated itself, and that time poor Aylwyn wasn't so lucky. It would have been different, you know, Jane, if he'd married a sensible girl with her feet on the ground, and strength of character that would have kept Aylwyn's feet there, too. But Silvia was as feather-headed as he was, they were just a pair of children. Heaven knows why she decided to marry him in the first place, perhaps she thought he had money; one can hardly believe that she was in love, leaving Aylwyn and the baby the way she did."

"Why didn't Aylwyn ever come back from Canada?"

"Because of Sinclair. Sometimes, the image of a father can be better than . . . the father himself. Sinclair is . . ." she corrected herself, with scarcely a tremor to her voice, "Sinclair was another Bailey. It's astonishing how a single bad trait will go right down through generations of the same family."

"You mean, all that gambling and stuff."

"Sinclair did talk to you, didn't he?"

"A little."

"There was no need for it, you know. He had a good job and a good salary, but he simply couldn't resist the thrill. And the fact that we don't understand it should never make us unsympathetic, although I sometimes think it was all Sinclair lived for."

"But he loved coming to Elvie."

"Only now and again. He didn't feel about it as your mother did . . . or you. In fact—" she turned her needles and started in on another row— "I decided some time ago, that it would be a good idea if Elvie should belong to you one day. Would you welcome that?"

"I . . . I don't know . . ."

"That was the real reason I was so anxious for your father to let you come home, and bombarded him with letters which the wretch refused to answer. I wanted to talk to you about Elvie."

I said, "It's a wonderful idea, but I'm scared of owning things . . . I don't think I'd want to be tied down by all the responsibilities of a place like Elvie. And I wouldn't be free to get up and go the way I'd want to."

"That sounds very chicken-hearted, and also a little like your father talking. If he'd been more realistic about possessions, he might have put down a few roots by now, and a good thing too. Don't you want roots, Jane? Don't you want to get married and have a family?"

I looked into the fire and thought of many things. Of Sinclair and my father . . . and David. And I thought of all the world I had seen, and the vast tracts of it which I hoped very much that one day I would see. And I thought of children at Elvie, my children, being brought up in this perfect place, and doing all the things that Sinclair and I had done . . .

I said at last, "I don't know what I want. And that's the truth."

"I didn't think you did. And today, when neither of us is in a frame of mind to be sensible about anything, is not the best time to discuss it. But you should think about it, Jane. Weigh up the pros and cons. There's all the time in the world to discuss it together."

A log broke, and fell into the smouldering embers of the fire. I got up to put on another, and while I was on my feet, stooped to pick up the tea tray, and carry it out to the kitchen, but as I reached the door, and stood, juggling with the tray and the door-handle, my grandmother spoke again.

"Jane."

"Yes."

Still holding the tray, I turned to face her. She had stopped knitting and now she took off her glasses, and I saw the blueness of her eyes, set deep in the pallor of her face. I had never seen her look so pale. I had never seen her look so old.

"Jane . . . do you remember, we were talking the other day, about Sinclair's friend, Tessa Faraday?"

My fingers closed over the handles of the tray and my knuckles showed white. I knew what was coming and prayed that it wouldn't. "Yes."

"I saw in the paper that she had died. Something about an overdose of barbiturates. Did you see that?"

"Yes, I did."

"You never said anything."

"No, I know."

"Was it . . . had it anything to do with Sinclair?"

Across the room, our eyes met and held. I would have given my soul at that moment to be able, convincingly, to lie. But I was incompetent, and my grandmother knew me very well. I hadn't a hope in hell of getting away with it.

I said, "Yes, it had." And then, "She was going to have his baby."

My grandmother's eyes filled with tears, and it was the only time I ever saw her cry.

Chapter 11

DAVID CAME the next afternoon. My grandmother was writing letters, and I had retreated to the garden and was sweeping up leaves, having once been told that physical toil is the best form of therapy for mental distress. I had made a small pile, and was about to transfer it to a handy wheelbarrow, when the french windows opened, and David came out to join me. I straightened to watch him cross the grass, all tall lankiness and wind-ruffled hair, and wondered in that moment how we would have got through the last few days without him. He had done everything, seen to everything, arranged everything, even finding time to put through a person-to-person call to my father, and tell him personally of Sinclair's death. And I knew that, whatever happened to the two of us, I should never cease being grateful to him.

He took the last bit of the bank in a single stride and was at my side. "Jane, what are you going to do with that little handful of leaves?"

"Put them into the barrow," I said, and did. They fluttered around, and most of them blew out again.

He said, "If you can lay your hands on a couple of bits of wood, you'll speed the process up considerably. I've brought you a letter . . ."

He took it out of his capacious pocket and I saw that it was from my father.

"How did you get this?"

"It was enclosed in one he wrote to me. He asked me to give it to you."

We abandoned the wheelbarrow and the broom, went down the garden, jumping the ha-ha into the field, and so on to the old jetty, where we settled ourselves, in some danger, side by side on the rotting boards, and I opened the letter and read it aloud to David.

"My darling Jane,

"I was so very sorry to hear about Sinclair and your involvement in his death, but glad that you were able to be with your grandmother, and no doubt of the greatest possible comfort to her.

"I feel guilty—and have been, ever since you went away—that I let you return to Elvie without putting you in the picture as regards your Uncle Aylwyn. But somehow, with one thing and another and the dramatic fashion in which you departed, the opportunity never presented itself. I did, however, mention it to David Stewart, and he promised to keep an eye on you and the general situation . . ."

I said, "But you never told me."

"It wasn't my business."

"But you knew."

"Of course I knew."

"And you knew about Sinclair as well?"

"I knew that he was getting through a hell of a lot of your grandmother's money."

"There's worse to come, David."

"What do you mean by that?"

"Sinclair died owing the most terrible amount."

"I was afraid that would happen. How did you know about this?"

"Because he told me. He told me lots of things." I went back to the letter.

"The reason that I was never over-anxious for you to return to Elvie was not so much what your Uncle had been, but what I was pretty sure your cousin Sinclair had become. After your mother died, your grandmother suggested that I should leave you with her, and indeed, this would have seemed to be the obvious answer. But there was the question of Sinclair. I knew how fond you were of him and how much he meant to you, and I was pretty sure that if you continued to see so much of him, the day would come when you would either have your heart broken, or your illusions shattered. Either process was bound to be painful, if not disastrous, and so instead, I kept you with me and brought you to America."

David interrupted. "I wonder what made him so sure about Sinclair."

I thought of the book, of Goldsmith's *Animated Nature*, and for a moment considered telling David the whole story. And then I decided against it. The book was no more. The day after Sinclair was killed, I retrieved it from his cupboard, took it downstairs and shovelled it into the boiler, where I watched it burn. Now, there was no trace left of it. Out of loyalty to Sinclair, it was best forgotten.

"I don't know . . . I suppose, instinct. He was always a very perceptive person, and impossible to fool." I went on reading:

"This was also the reason I was so tardy in replying to your grandmother's requests that you should return to Elvie. It would have been different if Sinclair were married, but I knew he wasn't and was devilled with apprehensions.

"I expect you will want to stay at Elvie for a bit, but business here has been fairly brisk. Sam Carter is doing great stuff for me, so I am in the money as the saying goes, and could even afford to buy you a ticket back to sunny California whenever you say the word. I miss you very much, and so does Rusty. Mitzi the poodle is small compensation for your absence, though Linda is determined that when the time is ripe and the moon in the right quarter, Mitzi and Rusty will fall madly in love and get themselves a family, but it is my considered opinion that the issue of such a union simply does not bear thinking about.

"Linda is well, adores Reef Point and what she calls the simple life, and has started, surprisingly, to paint. I don't know if my instincts are right or not, but I have a feeling that she may be very good. Who knows, she may yet be able to support me in the style to which I would like to be accustomed. Which is more than I could ever say for you.

"My love, darling child,
            from your father."

In silence I folded the letter, and put it back into its envelope, and so into the pocket of my coat. After a little, I said, slowly, "It sounds to me as though he's trying to talk her into marrying him. Or maybe she's trying to talk him into marrying her. I'm not sure which."

"Perhaps they're trying to talk each other. Would you like that to happen?"

"Yes, I think I would. Then I wouldn't feel responsible for him any longer. I'd be free."

The word had a disappointingly empty ring to it. It was very cold out on the jetty and suddenly I shivered, and David put an arm around me and drew me close into the warm circle of his arm, so that I was warmed by his warmth, my head supported by his solid tweed-clad shoulder.

"In that case," he said, "perhaps this is as good a time as any to start talking you into marrying a half-blind country lawyer who's adored you since the first moment he set eyes on you."

I said, "You wouldn't need to talk very hard."

His arm tightened and I felt his lips brush against the top of my head. "You wouldn't mind living in Scotland?"

"No. Provided you acquire yourself plenty of clients in New York, and California, and perhaps ever farther afield, and promise faithfully to take me with you whenever you go to see them."

"That shouldn't be too difficult."

"And it would be nice if I could have a dog."

"Of course you shall . . . not another Rusty, of course, he has to be unique. But perhaps one with the same interesting ancestry and equal intelligence and charm."

I turned in his arms, and buried my face in his chest. I thought for a dreadful moment that I was going to cry, but that was ridiculous, people didn't cry when they were happy, only in books. I said, "I love you," and David held me very close, and I did cry after all, but it didn't matter.

We sat there, wrapped around in David's coat, making unrealistic plans—like being married in the Reef Point Mission, and having Isabel Modes McKenzie knit me a wedding dress—which inevitably dissolved into laughter. So we abandoned them and made others, and so preoccupied were we that we did not notice the light fade, and the evening air grow chill. We were finally disturbed by my grandmother, opening the window and calling out to tell us that tea was ready, so we stood up, cramped and cold, and started back to the house.

The garden was bloomed with dusk and thick with shadows. We had not spoken again of Sinclair but all at once I felt him everywhere, not the man, but the boy I remembered. He ran, soft-footed, across the grass, and from the shadows beneath the trees came the soft scuffle of fallen leaves. And I wondered if Elvie would ever be free of him, and this made me sad, for whatever happened, and whoever lived there, I did not want it to be a haunted place.

David, going ahead of me, had stopped to collect my broom and the wheelbarrow and stow them, out of harm's way, under the maple. Now, he waited, his tall figure silhouetted against the lights of the house.

"What is it, Jane?"

I told him. "Ghosts."

"There aren't any," he said, and I looked again, and saw that he was right. Only sky and water, and the wind stirring the leaves. No ghosts. I went on and he took my hand in his, and together we went in to tea.